PLATINUM CANARY

PLATINUM CANARY

Ronald Tierney

This first world edition published in Great Britain 2005 by
SEVERN HOUSE PUBLISHERS LTD of
9–15 High Street, Sutton, Surrey SM1 1DF.
This first world edition published in the USA 2005 by
SEVERN HOUSE PUBLISHERS INC of
595 Madison Avenue, New York, N.Y. 10022.

British Library Cataloguing in Publication Data

Tierney, Ronald
    Platinum canary - (The Deets Shanahan mysteries)
    1.   Shanahan, Deets (Fictitious character) - Fiction
    2.   Private investigators - Indiana - Indianapolis - Fiction
    3.   Missing persons - California - San Francisco - Fiction
    4.   Detective and mystery stories
    I.   Title
    813.5'4 [F]

    ISBN 0-7278-6239-1

Typeset by Palimpsest Book Production Ltd.,
Polmont, Stirlingshire, Scotland.
Printed and bound in Great Britain by
MPG Books Ltd., Bodmin, Cornwall.

Dedicated to: Ryan Tierney, the Younger

"I got red wine and I got white wine. It's pretty well aged. The bottles have been here for thirty years 'cause nobody that comes into the bar wants a stinkin' glass of wine."

—Harry in his bar on 10th Street

One

E xcept for the gentle rise and fall of his chest, 71-year-old Dietrich Shanahan wasn't moving at all. A clear bottle of Miller High Life rested on the wide, flat arm of the white Adirondack chair on the little patch of green lawn of his backyard. The bottle, half full, perspired in the gentle May heat though the air contained not a drop of humidity. The weather, a pleasant 73 degrees under cloudless, blue skies, was a far cry from 13 below last March.

As Shanahan dreamed, Maureen worked. She propped up a drooping foxglove and plucked little leafy invaders from the flowerbed. Beyond, against the fence, budding irises, lilies, and puffs of white and pink peonies, and lilac bushes softened the landscape.

Sounds from a baseball game drifted incoherently through the screen door. A biplane, perhaps part of the downtown parade, disrupted the general sense of quiet for a moment and added to the timeless nature of the afternoon. A few seconds later, a car door slammed. A dog barked, and Casey, Shanahan's hound, opened his eyes for a moment before drifting away again in the warmth of the sun. The sounds remained distant, as if they were happening in a separate world.

A breeze swept through Maureen's long auburn hair. She stopped working, stood, guided a stray lock back from her face, let her eyes travel over their small private retreat in the city of Indianapolis and then to the sleeping detective. Satisfied with what she surveyed, she headed for the kitchen, struggling with desire. Would she be able to control it? No. In the kitchen, she opened a quart of her new favorite ice cream.

She felt disloyal to the Swiss Almond Vanilla she had loved for at least a decade. But Pistachio had won her 45-year-old heart.

"Change is good," she said to herself.

Shanahan's eyelids fluttered.

It was a dark dream. A silent dream. He could feel pine needles against his cheek. He could barely breathe. He could smell fertilizer and rotten leaves. He suffocated. His body deserted him, oozed into the earth. Nothing to hold on to. No voice came from his mouth, though the words made it to his throat.

He would have been gone had he not heard someone call his name. Again, then again.

He awoke with a start, relieved. He didn't know why he was relieved. He remembered nothing of the dream.

"Deets!" he heard Maureen call. He turned to look toward the house. She stood in the doorway. "Phone."

"You can eat your ice cream in front of me," Shanahan said, stepping inside the kitchen. He gave her a knowing smile.

"I can smell it on your breath," he said to her forced blank stare.

She pretended to be puzzled by his statement as he went toward the kitchen phone.

"There's ice cream on the scoop. It's not melted," he continued.

She remained quiet.

"There's an eyewitness," he said, looking down at the cat, Einstein, a walking bag of bones with the appetite of a lion. "He only comes in the kitchen when he hears the refrigerator door open."

She gave him the "you're a smart ass" smile.

"Why do you hide it?"

"It's fun. I like having secrets," she said. She opened the freezer, pulled out the container, a spoon sunk deep into the contents.

"Yes," Shanahan said into the receiver.

"Another forbidden joy exposed," she muttered to herself. "What is there to live for?"

"Hello?" Shanahan said a little louder, hearing the dial tone. "Male or female?" he asked Maureen as he placed the old Princess-style wall phone back in its cradle.

"Male."

"He asked for me, specifically?"

"If you are the only Mr. Shanahan living here, then I guess it was specifically." She gave him a fake smile. "Maybe if you had answered the phone rather than interrogate me for a victimless crime . . ."

The phone rang again sometime in the middle of the night. Shanahan, in bed, answered it, groggily, repeating hello three times. After the third he heard a click and a dial tone.

"Who was it?" came the soft voice of the woman beside him.

"Same person who called earlier, I think."

The fluorescent light rained down on the aisles of the 24-hour Marsh Supermarket on Keystone and Broad Ripple Avenue. The light turned human flesh a faint shade of lime, made all the eerier by the folks who shop at 3 A.M. These were bartenders, emergency-room workers, firefighters, exotic dancers, cops and the others who either worked odd hours or perhaps insomniacs—all decent folks, Cross was sure, during regular hours, but who seemed zombiesque at this late and lonely hour.

Howie Cross was a private investigator, who had just trailed a wayward husband from a strip joint to his driveway. The evening had ended and Cross was hungry.

But the place was so huge—aisles and aisles of cans and boxes. He didn't know where to start. Produce? No, he thought. Lettuce? Green beans? No. He didn't want anything fresh or healthful. He wanted something heavy to deaden his mind, bring him down from his caffeine dodginess, nudge him toward sleep. He found himself in the frozen-food section, flirting with a package of Fettuccini Alfredo when he saw a guy in a long gray coat and a stocking cap. Too warm out, even in the middle of the night, for a coat like that. Another problem. The guy walked stiff-legged. Was he lame or was there a shotgun stuffed down the leg of his pants? Could be trouble.

He put the box of frozen food back in the compartment and inched his way to get a closer look. When the guy turned back to face Cross, it was clear, he wasn't set to rob the place. Beneath the gray whiskers, was an old face. A very old face. There was no anger, no madness in the eyes. Puzzlement perhaps. Resignation for sure. His shoes were worn through. Cross could see a bit of the dirty green sock in the hole of the tattered running shoes. He walked feebly and Cross doubted the old guy was steady enough to hold to anything he might want to pilfer. The guy was homeless or close to it. The old guy was looking at the abundance of food the way a guy on a clerk's salary smudged the windows of a BMW dealer.

The old vagrant might pilfer a box of crackers, but he was going to do no one any harm.

So there you are, Howie said to himself. You never really were a cop and you're still not a civilian. When the Indianapolis Police Department had asked him to consider a new career, he'd been relieved. He hated arresting kids for having a bag of weed. He hated arresting prostitutes when, if anything, they were the victims. He didn't like the idea that a guy who stole a canned ham could be sent up, but a guy who stole from his own employee retirement accounts would get off by simply paying a fine from the funds he stole. A bag of pot could get you twenty years in some places. Swindle investors and employees out of their retirement and live in luxury.

So while Cross wasn't cut out to be on the police force, he wasn't exactly right for the corporate world either. He gravitated—or sank, possibly—to the margins of society. He followed men who lie to their wives or wives who lie to their husbands. Was that any better? Probably not, but all he did was try to tell people the truth.

He went back for the frozen Alfredo. Hey, life was good, wasn't it? He'd have a great Italian meal. A frozen dinner, a $6.99 bottle of Pinot Grigio, and if he was lucky maybe a rerun of *I Love Lucy*.

Shanahan awoke, the solitary inhabitant of the bed and the bedroom. It was an unusual situation. Usually he was up well before she was. He would feed the animals, grind the coffee, pick up the *Indianapolis Star* from the front porch, read Dan Carpenter's column, followed by the National League baseball scores, and the editorial section, all before Maureen made her first groggy appearance.

He slipped on a pair of pants, his shirt, slippers, and entered into the quiet of the little two-bedroom bungalow, then into the sunny kitchen. No nervous clamor from the animals. He went to the open door, looked through the screen. Maureen sat out in back, in the Adirondack, a cup of coffee in her hand.

She was beautiful, he thought. He looked at the clock above the stove. 10 A.M. How did that happen? He felt rested. As he aged, he slept less. These days, he rarely slept more than five hours. What was different about last night?

The phone rang.

"Yes," Shanahan said curtly. Most of his calls were from telemarketers.

"Is this Mr. Shanahan?"

"It is."

"Can I talk to you?"

"We are talking," Shanahan said.

"I mean business. Somewhere."

"Who is this?"

"My name is Todd."

"Todd who?"

There was a pause. "Evans. Todd Evans."

"What's this about?"

"I'd rather talk to you in person. Is that possible?"

5

"When?"

"Today."

"Just so we're straight here," Shanahan said, "you're interested in the services of a private detective?"

"Yes . . . I mean I think so. That's what I want to talk about."

"Where?"

"Somewhere public," Todd said. His voice was young and anxious.

Shanahan wavered. He wasn't getting much from the guy. Why should he venture out on the chance that the guy would even show up?

"You called last night, right?" Shanahan said.

"Yeah, I'm sorry."

"Why did you hang up?"

"I wasn't sure I wanted to go through with this."

"What changed your mind?"

"Something's changed," he said.

They made arrangements to meet at noon at Shanahan's regular haunt, a bar on 10th Street. Todd could break away from work for lunch. They would talk then.

"You OK?" Shanahan asked Maureen.

She looked up, smiled. "Couldn't sleep," she said.

"Are you unhappy?"

"No, no, not really. Time seems to be running out."

"For what? To get what done?"

"I wish I knew." She looked up, then stood. "I'm all right, Deets. A little fleeting melancholy. I dreamt of my parents. They were very sweet, very warm. They wanted me to like them. Forgive them. Very strange." She grabbed her coffee and headed toward the house. "And you! You slept the sleep of innocence."

"My second childhood," Shanahan said. "It's *lovely*."

Shanahan arrived at the bar at eleven thirty, half an hour before his noon appointment and before Harry officially opened the doors.

6

A slight man, getting slighter in his advancing years, Harry looked like the kind of guy who'd never looked young. Wrinkled face, squinty eyes, hairy ears. He was feisty, funny, loyal, disagreeable, tough and such a romantic at heart that he'd married seven times.

Light swept in through the open door, making the small bar look even shabbier than it did in its naturally dimly lit state. Harry grumbled something about something as he walked ahead of Shanahan.

"What?" Shanahan called after him.

"I tried to call you last night," Harry said.

"Out to dinner. The worst food I've ever tasted," Shanahan said. "You'd love it."

"Van broke down," Harry said. "You should get a cell phone."

"I don't like cell phones."

"I don't like busted radiators. So? Why can't I count on you?"

"I'm sorry, I thought I gave you up for adoption when you were twelve."

Harry began to grind the coffee beans. "What are you doing here anyway?" he yelled over the sound.

"Business, you remember what that is, don't you." He looked down the empty bar.

"I remember to mind my own business," Harry said.

The large-screen television was blank, resting on a shelf, high up, at the far end of the bar. A voluptuous nude reclined somewhat comically in the poster above the bar.

It wouldn't be long before the neighborhood regulars would find their regular stools and sit, drinking away, one slow hour after another, one more day of their lives.

Once upon a time, not too long ago, Shanahan owned one of those stools, the one closest to the door. It was his for decades. There he downed countless bottles of Miller High Life and shots of J. W. Dant Olde Bourbon. Without comment, without emotion, without conscious thought, he mourned the sudden, unexpected departure of his wife and son. There were

7

short reprieves, of course, the Cubs' games, a hand of poker now and then, Harry's stories, and Delaney's famous stew, before Delaney sold the bar to Harry and left Harry with a decoy recipe. It wasn't until Maureen came along that he did more than merely accept life as an uninspired duty.

"Pretty good, Deets. You tell me I'm a poor businessman and then you expect me to provide you office space here free of charge."

"I rest my case."

Two

At noon, Todd walked in. If Harry's regular crowd had assembled, they'd have taken notice. The tall, thirty-ish black man was wearing a suit. You never saw a suit in Harry's little saloon. A uniform maybe—police, maintenance, hospital scrubs and maybe UPS. But not a real suit. It wasn't a really expensive suit, Shanahan judged, but a nice one off the rack that hung elegantly on the frame of the slender young man. He looked out of place. He seemed to feel it too.

"It's pretty run down," Shanahan said gesturing to the surroundings. He extended his hand. "But it's home."

Todd took the hand hesitantly. Shanahan recognized the look that came with the shake. "I had no idea you'd be this old" was written across his face.

"Despite what you think, you and I are about the same age," Shanahan said, "but I've lived a much harder life."

Todd smiled, took a seat next to Shanahan at the bar.

"Something to drink?" Shanahan said loud enough for Harry to hear.

"Coke maybe."

"Why is it you called me instead of someone with a big ad in the *Yellow Pages*?" Shanahan asked.

"Jennifer Bailey," Todd said. "You know her, right?"

Shanahan nodded. He did. He'd worked for her a few times when she was still taking criminal cases. Now she was Attorney General for the State of Indiana.

"She recommended you." He thought a moment, measuring his words. "I'm seeing . . . was seeing her niece."

"Jasmine?" Shanahan asked.

9

"Sister. Lianna."

"And?"

"Lianna is gone. Missing. Something. I don't know."

"How long has she been gone?"

"I don't know. It could be a week, but maybe only a few days."

"Is that right? Could be this. Could be that."

Harry set a glass of cola on the bar. Todd waited for him to leave before picking up the conversation.

"We had a fight. She wasn't speaking to me. I tried to find her on the weekend. Her parents are long gone. I called her aunt. She hadn't heard from her. Her best friend didn't know where she was. Her cell phone rings. No one answers."

"Maybe she wants to do some serious thinking and went away for a few days."

"I know something's happened. I knew that yesterday, which is why I called you, but thoughts like 'she just wanted some time alone to sort things out' made me doubt how I feel. This morning I talked with a person she works with. Lianna didn't show up for work. She didn't call in. They were concerned too. She has a really good job. She'd never do anything like that."

"You've called the police?"

"No."

Shanahan knew they wouldn't do much about it this soon anyway.

"You call the hospitals?"

"Yes. Nothing." He looked at Shanahan expectantly.

"Why were you fighting?"

"It's really pretty personal."

"We'll need to get a whole lot more personal than that, I'm afraid."

"She wanted to break it off. Move out." Todd looked away.

"And you?" Shanahan asked.

"I wanted . . . I was the first to talk about breaking up . . . but I changed my mind."

"Are you sure this isn't some little game you guys are

playing? Making each other pay for hurting each other?"

"She's pregnant," Todd said with barely concealed anger.

"Is that why you wanted to break up?"

"That's why I didn't."

"Could she be in a clinic somewhere?"

"No. She can't . . . wouldn't do that." He looked at Shanahan as if something or someone struck him. His body seemed to collapse into itself. "In so many words, what she said was that she wanted the baby, but she didn't want me."

"In so many words? What were her exact words?"

"I don't remember. I remember her meaning."

Before Todd left to get back to work, Shanahan learned a few more things about the young man and the missing woman. Todd was a graduate of Purdue University. He worked at Masters, Credlin and Hawkins as an investment analyst. He and Lianna shared an apartment in the lofts built in the old Real Silk factory in a charming revitalized area near downtown. Lianna worked as an executive assistant to the CEO of one of the largest pharmaceutical companies in the country. Both had good jobs. Until recently they were saving to buy a new home and planned to have children when the time was right.

"Will you find her?" Todd had asked as he looked at his watch and prepared to leave. "Try, I mean."

"I'll call you. Let me make some calls first, then we'll see."

The regulars had descended on Harry's place before Todd left and they were wide-eyed and curious.

"It's amazing," Harry said, "having someone in here not on Social Security. I like it." He grinned. "Maybe I could turn this place into a hip joint."

"A hip-replacement joint maybe," Shanahan said as he leaned over the bar, to retrieve a thick telephone book. He put on his glasses, trying desperately to see in the dim light of the bar.

Harry brought him a flashlight, and pulled the bar phone over to Shanahan's spot at the bar.

"And you are being so nice to me because?" Shanahan asked.

"Aren't I always nice to you?"

"No."

"You have such a suspicious mind. It's a shame, that's what it is." He put on a face of deep hurt.

Shanahan dialed. "Could I speak with Jennifer Bailey. Tell her it's Shanahan."

"I'm sorry, she has someone in her office, can I take a message?" said the male voice. He gave her the number at the bar. The Cubs were playing an afternoon game. Harry had already switched it on. He'd wait for the call.

Jennifer Bailey called during the third inning.

"I've been talking with young Todd Evans."

"I gave him your name."

"I know. What do you think?" Shanahan asked.

"I gave him your name for two reasons," she said. "One, I want to find Lianna and I will supplement any of the fees necessary to do that. Two, I want someone I can trust to do the right thing, no matter what that right thing is."

"Meaning, you think he might be asking to find someone he doesn't want found?"

"Possibly."

"You have special reason to believe that?"

"Nothing more than the fact that the boyfriend is always a suspect in cases like these."

"Why hasn't anyone called the police?"

"No one has officially called them. But I've talked with Lt. Swann in Homicide," Bailey said. "We don't even know if it's a homicide and I rack my brain at some sort of other explanation, but I want a jump on whatever it is. What I'm saying is, the police are on it, unofficially at this point."

Shanahan knew that Jennifer Bailey, as Attorney General, could make those kinds of requests. She had the power. Because it was personal and she was an elected official, she wouldn't want to exercise it too publicly. Shanahan also knew Swann. She contacted the right guy. He was low-key, responsible, and honest.

"Will they be upset if they know I'm poking around too?"

"I'll make a call. Does this mean you're taking the case?"

"Yes, now that I've talked to you."

"What do you think of him?" she asked.

"Don't know. How about you?"

"I liked him a lot, Mr. Shanahan. If something happened to her and he was involved, I would consider that two tragedies. But they were having a rough time. There were some passionate differences. We should talk. Is it possible for you to meet me at the Westin for a drink at five thirty? It would be nice to see you again."

Shanahan agreed to meet with her at the bar near the Statehouse. He called Maureen to say they'd each be on their own for dinner.

"Hot date?" Maureen asked.

"Yes, with a beautiful woman."

"Dinner?"

"Drinks."

"Good, then I can spend some time with the pool boy."

"We don't have a pool."

"Then I guess we'll just have to do something else with our time."

Cross woke up at 4 P.M. Earlier, that morning, one glass of wine had led to another, or maybe one bottle had led to another. The only thing unusual about it was that it was wine, not harder stuff. He didn't have a hangover. Never did. Just felt as if he hadn't slept at all and that there wasn't a drop of liquid anywhere in his body.

He finally persuaded himself to take a shower, after which he would drink a pot of coffee, fully aware that wouldn't help him rehydrate. Next he would sit himself down in front of his little iMac computer and write the report for his client.

Mrs. Channing hired him to find out what Mr. Channing was doing when he "worked late." Something was always "coming up," she told him and she was pretty sure she knew what it was. She didn't have a fat bank account; so they settled on a plan for Cross to tail him on random evenings for a month. For the money, he would do seven nights. He had one more night to go.

13

So far it appeared that on three of those nights he did work late and went out with the boys afterward. On the other three, he worked late and then hit a strip bar on Lafayette Road. So, her husband wasn't seeing another woman, he was seeing other women; but likely as not he was only *seeing* them, perhaps getting a lap dance or two.

Was that cheating? Not up to Cross to decide. He'd never been married. Didn't seem to be in his future, either.

Relationships were tough. Until last month, Cross thought he had something with Melanie Dart. Turned out he didn't. A couple of years ago he had a more intense affair with a dancer. It didn't end well either. In most of the relationships he had with women—unsuccessful, all of them—it was Cross who would come to feel suffocated, owned, and trapped. It was Cross who resented probing questions about his past, his feelings, his expectations about the future.

All of that was turned on its head with Melanie Dart. Cross couldn't help it. It was his nature to ask questions. To find out everything. She was the one who felt suffocated and moved on.

But there was another "M" in his life. Margot.

It was worse with Margot. He'd never felt so jealous, so needy. As painful as it was to break up, he grew to understand it would have been disastrous to both of them to continue. Maybe Margot understood what was going on better than he did at the time. Maybe she broke it off because she could see what it was doing to him. Was she being noble or what? They would never have a regular life.

The hot shower reawakened nerve endings, and put a little light in his soggy brain. He looked at himself in the mirror as he dried himself off. Remarkable, how he held up. Lots of bad habits. No good ones. He looked fit. It must be the genes, he thought.

Cross sat at the computer, opened the file on Lester C. Channing, typed in yesterday's date below the previous entry and described as he'd learned to do on police reports the man's actions from 5 P.M. until 2:30 A.M. this morning.

Three

Shanahan always felt like an old broom when he was in the company of Jennifer Bailey. Not that he felt like he deserved the likes of Maureen either, but the two were very different people. Maureen was like a wild Irish Rose, an unrestrained beauty in every sense of the word, yet vulnerable under a tougher facade. Jennifer Bailey—and Shanahan could never bring himself to call her just "Jennifer," even in his mind—was quite the opposite. Refined, elegant, soft-spoken, and tough. She'd have to have been tough to build her own very successful law firm, and then to become the state's attorney general. That would be a challenge for anyone. More so for a woman. And even more than that for a black woman in this not quite northern state.

Jennifer Bailey was waiting, sipping a Martini. She smiled as Shanahan approached.

"It's been a long time since we've actually seen each other," she said.

Shanahan nodded and sat across from her.

"How's Maureen?"

"Wonderful," he said.

The quiet that followed wasn't uneasy, but it reminded both of them that the nature of their relationship over the years was, while respectful, almost purely business. She seemed to pick that up.

"Thank you for looking into this matter," she continued. "Are you going to be able to do your usual thorough job with what he's able to pay you?"

"At least for awhile."

"You have a place to start?"

"I'll make arrangements to go through her things, check out phone calls, other bills, talk to her friends, see where all of that takes me. Then I'll have a better idea."

"I hope this isn't terrible for you . . ." she began, but was interrupted by the waiter who presented a friendly enquiring face.

"Miller," Shanahan said, then remembered there were Lites and Drafts and who knows how many else. "The real one."

"I hope you don't mind me inserting myself in your investigation, in Todd's," she said, "but I love my niece and it's possible that I might be able to help if I know what's going on."

Shanahan had to think about it. "Let's let Todd know, then I'll be fine."

"That's why I like working with you," she said. "You're a dying breed. An honorable man," she added quickly to clear up the meaning.

"Anything else you can tell me about her? I have Todd's perspective."

She took a small sip of her Martini, then took a deep breath.

"Let's see. Smart. Headstrong. Beautiful and knew it; but was reluctant to use it."

"Ambitious?"

"Yes, very much like her aunt. We were very much alike, except for the beautiful part."

"Not true."

"Which part isn't true?" A faint smile crossed her lips, then her face turned sad. "She lights up a room when she comes into it. She has incredible energy. I can't imagine her not being here."

"She has no faults?"

"Yes. She really had to have her way. What is it that people say now? 'My way or the highway.' She's not reticent about anything. Though I'm sure she can be diplomatic at work. She'd have to be, in her day-to-day life, though she's not likely to suffer fools lightly."

"How was she ambitious?"

"She knew what she wanted. She had a degree in business, a masters in chemistry, and was working on her doctorate. She wanted to be CEO of a Fortune 500 pharmaceutical company by the time she was thirty-five. Her boss at Noah Rose and Company was mentoring her. She kept getting raises, big ones. She's the kind of person who demands to have her share of whatever it is. I think the way she was could be pretty frustrating to any man in her life."

"And that means Todd?"

Jennifer Bailey nodded.

"And I'm not sure how he felt about how her salary and career, I suppose, was eclipsing his own."

Kind of a double whammy, Shanahan thought. The two of them talked about Lianna and Todd and eventually the conversation turned to memories of their past work together. He asked about Jasmine. Was she still with the young man so sorely addicted to heroin?

"They're still working it out. Thanks for your help. And here you are again. I do so much appreciate you." She patted him on the hand.

Shanahan suddenly felt foolish sitting so casually at the table. If something had happened to Lianna, he needed to move on it right away.

"I need to get over to Todd and Lianna's place," he said, standing. "I'll go make a call."

"Use this," she said, reaching in her purse for a slender aluminum cell phone. He flipped it open, but didn't know what to do next.

She smiled, took it back, punched in the numbers and then handed it back to Shanahan.

"I haven't got a microwave either," he said as the phone rang. A dying breed, he thought.

Cross pulled himself together. He'd try to get to Channing's building by seven just in case the man left earlier than usual.

Channing's black Ford van, with the company name,

Universal Security, in huge yellow letters on the sides, was parked up by the front door where it usually resided. Cross parked across and down the street. Plenty of spaces. His own, dirty sedan blended in nicely with the gaggle of other cars in the area. He would wait.

Pretty ambitious, Cross thought. He'd heard of City Security, State Security and National Security, but Universal Security—doesn't get any bigger than that. And such a crummy building. The firm, which Channing owned, installed burglar alarms, and farmed out security guard requests through another, larger company. Security could be a pretty sleazy business, much like his own.

Unlike previous nights he didn't have to sit long, staring at the dead and dreary street.

Channing came out. Alone this time. He was a big guy, barrel-chested. He wore a suit that was a little too tight and gave away the weapon strapped to his belt in back. He carried a manila envelope.

Cross waited. He let the van turn the corner before he pulled out.

It was a ten-minute drive to the Palace of Gold's strip club. Cross slowly pulled into the parking lot and watched as Channing's van negotiated a back-in to a small space.

Cross pulled in a spot closer to the exit. He debated whether or not to go in. He hadn't during Channing's first stop. He didn't want to inflate his client's bill with a cover charge and expensive drinks—not to mention at least a few obligatory tips. He noticed the 5x7 envelope tucked into the side pocket of Channing's suit. He'd go in. Maybe he should see if Channing was there for business or pleasure. He waited a couple of minutes, letting Channing settle before making his entrance.

Cross wore a pair of jeans, a sweatshirt and a baseball cap. During previous outings, he'd worn a sports coat and glasses. Nothing that would fool his mother, but just changing the image enough that a stranger couldn't get a lock on him. He'd even changed cars—now driving an old Volvo he borrowed from Sam's Blue Ribbon Autos. Cross worked with Sam on repossessions and a few hours in one of the cars off the lot were part of the deal.

Inside the Palace of Gold were a dozen or so guys, most of them solo, sipping on beers, staring at a redhead on the stage in the center of the space. Pale and lightly freckled suggesting that the red hair might be real, the dancer came on stage wearing the legal minimum—pasties and a T-back thong. The music was a rousing rock 'n' roll that Cross couldn't identify. The Allman Brothers?

She was a little too voluptuous for Cross, so it wasn't hard to scan the room, to check out Channing, who sat at a table. Cross went to the bar. The way they angled, the best Channing could do was to get a partial profile of the guy following him.

When the redhead moved off the stage, a tall, leggy black woman took the stage. She wore a silver blond wig, had a silver blond boa. Silver, tasseled pasties covered the nipples of her perfectly proportional breasts, and a gauzy silver "V" barely covered what must legally be covered between her very long legs. Silver sparkles covered her eyelids and lips. She was all show business, all sensational, Cross thought.

"Whoa boy," he told himself as the bartender finally came up to enquire about his intentions to drink.

Cross ordered a Newcastle Ale and reminisced about his two exciting but, in the end, disastrous experiences with dancers. One was smart as a whip and crazy as a loon. The other's obsession with meth didn't mesh with Howie's cravings for alcohol. Number two was painful. He wouldn't go through it again. He'd sworn off.

He sipped slowly. He was on duty and he didn't want to run up the bill. The redhead was making her rounds of the guys at tables.

Cross knew the routine.

"Hope you don't mind," the girl would say, sitting at the table. She'd ask questions. Either, "Are you from here?" Or, "I haven't seen you here before?"

A waitress would come by the table. If the guy offered to

buy the dancer a drink, she'd stay. If he didn't, she'd move on. If she stayed, she got a piece of the price of the drink, and she would steer the conversation toward business. Would he like a lap dance? A couch dance? There was also a VIP room in these places where the girls go further than the law allows, where sometimes no one gets caught and the guys are relieved of their stress and their greenbacks.

A fair exchange, Cross always thought, as long as the girls chose the business they were in.

After the third song, the feathery ebony-skinned dancer descended and moved directly to Channing's table. She sat as if she was expected. They talked. Cross couldn't read lips— at least not in this light—but he could read attitude and body language. He didn't see the usual seductive pouts and poses. The conversation was serious. She nodded, sadly, it seemed. He tried to hand her the envelope. She pushed it away, shaking her head "no." She nodded toward the back of the room. She said something and, instead of making her rounds, Channing followed her through a doorway.

A special show in the VIP lounge? Cross wondered. Why the envelope? Drugs, he thought. Could be drugs. Meth. Cocaine. Channing as a pusher or was that the price she asked for whatever it is they were going to do? All speculation. Truth was, Cross didn't know.

He waited. He sat through three new silicone-enhanced dancers before the redhead reappeared. Cross looked around. Channing hadn't reemerged. His table had been cleaned.

Cross felt his stomach suddenly sink. "Jesus H. Christ," he shouted, causing the room and the dancer to stare at him. He shrugged his shoulders in apology, slapped down another five on the bar and went out front. The van was gone. Completely and utterly gone. The back door. He knew about back doors. How could he have let this happen?

Cross didn't know where to go now. He took a chance and drove by Channing's house. No luck. Perhaps on this last night of his investigation, Cross had blown it. Maybe this was the night he was going to do whatever it was his wife suspected he'd do. Maybe he left with her. No couch dance. No VIP rooms. Something more comfortable, perhaps more leisurely.

"So be it," Cross said.

Tonight he would wrap up the investigation, finish the report, collect his meager wages, and not worry for a day or two about how he was going to make the car payments and the mortgage.

Todd gave Shanahan a sad scowl and nodded toward the living room. Inside was Lieutenant Swann, from IPD. Scattered on the cocktail table in front of the sofa were bills, a checkbook, bank statements, and other assorted pieces of paper. Swann looked up, nodded.

"This is unofficial," Swann said. "Trying to get a head start in case it starts to go bad." He looked at Todd. "Can you let me into her email account?"

Todd led him to a desk in the bedroom. A slender laptop computer was open, the screen was lit. Shanahan followed.

"You can get into her account?"

"Yes," Todd said, and sat. He clicked on the screen, then typed in LiannaBailey and another word Shanahan couldn't make out because it showed on the screen as asterisks. In seconds, the screen flashed back a list.

"Could you print that out for me?" Swann said. "Let's look at the trash and the outbox. Also drafts." He turned to Shanahan as Todd performed the requested tasks. "I'm taking the phone bills and bank statements." He was quiet for a moment. There was nothing Shanahan could say; though he'd like to say he didn't like getting stiffed for the information. Fortunately, he didn't have to. "I'll make you copies," Swann said.

"Thanks."

"Let's work together."

"When I can," Shanahan said.

Swann didn't press it. Instead he leaned down so that his face was close to Todd's. Todd stopped what he was doing.

"Mr. Evans, if you have already, or plan to do anything to

21

this computer to erase, dump, or manipulate data, you'll be in deep shit."

Swann said it calmly without the macho inflections, but it was clear he meant it and it was clear Todd was shaken by the not so subtle accusation.

"I have no reason to do that, Lieutenant Swann. I want her back." Todd was trying to be forceful, but his voice broke.

Swann gathered all the papers. Todd glared at him. "I could take the computer too," Swann threatened in response.

"Not without a warrant," Shanahan said. "You probably shouldn't be taking what you're taking, but we do appreciate your working on this unofficially, don't we, Todd?"

Todd nodded.

"Have I ever treated you bad?" Swann asked Shanahan.

"No. I mean it. I'm glad you're helping. But it's pretty early to jump to any conclusions."

"OK, let's work together, all right?" he said, giving Shanahan another querying look.

Shanahan nodded.

"In these kinds of cases, we don't have a lot of time. We're probably too late now," Swann said and left.

Todd shut the door, then nearly collapsed back against it. He shook his head. "What did he mean it was too late now."

"It's best to get a jump on missing persons. It gets harder as time passes."

"You think she's been harmed?" Todd asked.

"We don't know. We need to look in every direction."

"He's accusing me," Todd said.

"Listen, you need to stay strong. Most crimes against another person are committed by family members, lovers, or friends. Every cop that's been on duty for more than a day and a half knows that. He has to keep you in the mix."

"And you?"

"Blank slate," Shanahan said. "I meant what I said about their help. The police have resources I couldn't begin to offer." Shanahan moved to the sofa and sat down. "Now, let's you and I talk about your last conversation before she disappeared and what she might have taken with her."

Shanahan learned a few more things about Todd and Lianna before he left. Shanahan learned that she left after they argued about the relationship. She wanted it to cool off for awhile. Maybe a trial separation. He didn't want her to move out. He felt as if he were losing her and their child.

"Was the fight physical?"

"No. No. Never. We didn't even yell," he said. "At least I don't think we did."

Shanahan asked what she took with her.

"Her purse," Todd said. "That was it."

"What was in her purse?"

Todd thought for a moment. "Cosmetics, wallet, brush, cell phone. I think, keys, I don't know."

"Car keys?"

"Yes. A silver Acura."

"Where is it?"

"The car?" Todd asked, then understood. "Gone. I told all of this to Lieutenant Swann before you got here."

"What was she wearing?"

"Jeans, running shoes, a T-shirt. It wasn't like she planned to go out."

"Jewelry."

"A ring. A watch. A pendant," he said. His eyes were closed as he spoke.

"Tell me about them."

"The pendant has a small cross on a thin chain," Todd said, still concentrating on something inside his brain. "The watch was the one she wore when she played tennis. Has a red band. I don't know the brand. Not expensive."

"And the ring?" Shanahan asked, relieved that the young man was using the present tense.

"Our engagement ring. Not a big diamond. Yellow diamond."

"Tell me what happened right before she left," Shanahan asked.

"What do you mean?"

"Did she run out? Did she say goodbye? Did she say she'd be back?"

"No. She just stopped talking. She looked at her watch and then just stopped talking. She gave me an expression I did not understand. It could have been sad, could have been confused. It was like she had a decision she couldn't make."

"Then she left."

"Then she left," Todd said confirming the statement.

"What did you think when she didn't come back?"

"I felt horrible, but I wasn't worried about her safety. She has friends, relatives. I figured she needed time alone. I thought she'd be back by now. I'm hoping that's still the case."

"Would she do this to punish you or to get attention?"

"Punish maybe. She didn't need to do anything like that to get attention. But I can't see her not letting someone know. Certainly she wouldn't jeopardize her career over this."

"Anything else gone? Luggage?"

Todd shook his head "no."

"Personal possessions? Photographs, favorite trinkets?"

"I don't know for sure. I don't think so."

"Check it out. I want to know if there is anything else missing."

Just beyond where Shanahan parked his car was the wonderful old Indianapolis neighborhood, Lockerbie. Lovely old restored homes, some of them quite nice. Big trees. Stone streets. It was a quiet evening. Warm. The stars were visible. There were a few people out walking, airing out their dogs, getting a breath of fresh spring air. Pleasant. Funny how one person can suffer a serious tragedy and the world goes on. And on.

Four

When Cross made it back to his place, after circling Channing's home and business, he found Channing's van parked in front. Channing himself sat on the concrete steps that led up through the trees to the former chauffeur's quarters that was now the detective's abode.

Channing smiled as Cross approached.

"Can I help you?" Cross said, though in his heart he knew he'd been caught. In his mind, he prayed that Channing wasn't too upset. He was a big, big man. Big head, big shoulders, big arms, big chest . . .

"Yeah." Channing came to his feet and was very imposing, standing a few steps higher than the ground Cross stood upon. "How much is my wife paying you?"

"Listen, I'm kind of in an ethical no man's land here." He was giving Channing the "help a guy out" and "I'm just doing my job" attitude.

Channing came down the steps slowly. His body language didn't suggest violent intent. But you never knew. People who could stay cool with their anger were more dangerous than those filled with spit and bluster.

"How long have you been tailing me?"

"This was my seventh and last night. I blew it tonight."

"No shit," Channing said, shaking his head in disbelief. "I usually spot 'em on the first day, usually right off the bat. You're good."

"Thanks. Looks to me like I could have been just a little bit better."

He nodded. "I've had some practice. I was twenty years with the Cincinnati Department."

"Got your retirement, good," Cross said.

"Add on a little social security, perhaps some investments. You know, live halfway decent when the time comes. Even had some property set up, but decided I'm just about ready to leave the Indiana winters for some place warm. You?"

"Struggling to get through the week," Cross said, trying to buy a little charity. "What was your beat?"

"From patrolman to Vice to Narcotics, finally Homicide. I got pretty good at tailing and knowing when I was tailed. What's your background?"

"Cop," Cross said.

"Figures. How long were you on?"

"Eleven years."

Channing scratched his ear and Cross braced himself. But Channing's ear apparently needed scratching. "Why didn't you go for the guaranteed golden years?"

"Wasn't up to me."

"On the take?"

"Listen, I appreciate your taking this like you are, but I'm not ready to be best friends."

Channing laughed. His big chest heaved and his belly rolled. He looked a little out of shape, but anyone that big—probably 280—had enough muscle underneath to do some damage. It took serious strength just to carry that much beef around.

"You've been picking my bones now for seven days. I don't even know what you know about me and, on top of that, my little friend, I'm going to be paying you for doing it. Now, don't you think you owe five minutes of polite conversation?"

"I didn't like the politics," Cross said. "I sometimes thought the cops were the bad guys."

"Interesting," Channing said. "You looking for work?"

"Maybe."

"Man, you are one cautious bastard," Channing said, shaking his head again. "I sometimes need help. It's that simple."

"We can talk about it," Cross said. Even after seven days

of surveillance, Cross didn't really have a clue about Channing, what kind of guy he was, who he was connected to, and how he viewed life. These things came to be important.

"What's your name?" Channing asked.

"Cross."

"First or last?"

"Last."

"All right, all right, what's your first name?" Channing's smile of amusement continued. He enjoyed quizzing the guy who tailed him. Trying to find a way to make him squirm.

Cross was aware of that. He was also aware that it would be petty not to answer such a seemingly innocuous question. Then again, he hated to give his first name. He hated the name "Howard." Though his nickname wasn't so bad when he was fourteen, a man of forty shouldn't be called "Howie."

"Howie."

"Howie. I'll be damned." Channing's laugh descended from his face to his belly. He was having fun now. It wasn't so much the words, but the superior attitude. Cross knew the game from his time with the IPD. Channing was acting the dominant dog—showing Cross who was in charge.

"So, *Howie*, what did you find out about me?"

"Not nearly enough. Raised more questions than answers."

"Like what, *Howie*?"

"Like what does it cost for you to get your rocks off in the VIP Lounge?" Cross asked.

"What?" Channing said.

"I saw you try to give her an envelope," Cross said.

Channing smiled, but it wasn't full of humor. His eyes said something else entirely. And it wasn't nice.

"I mean, what does it cost for a guy like you to actually get sex?" There it was. He might have to pay for that remark. His body language or maybe just the furtive movement of his eyes must have given him away.

"I'm not going to hit you, Howie. I don't pick on Cub Scouts."

Channing went to his van, turned back after opening the door.

27

"Hey, and forget the job offer, OK, pal. You wouldn't cut it."

"How was your date?" Maureen asked when Shanahan came back. She put her book, a thick one by Margaret Atwood, down on the pillow of the sofa beside her.

"Sweet," Shanahan said.

"What did you have to eat?"

Shanahan smiled. Even if he were having an affair with someone, she'd be more interested in where they dined and what they ordered than in anything else.

"I didn't," he said, suddenly feeling ravenous.

"You want me to fix you something?"

"No, I'll do something."

He went into the kitchen, put a pot of hot water on the stove. He chopped up some garlic very fine and tossed it into a small pan along with some butter and turned on the gas with the flame so low, it would go out if it were any lower.

Maureen came in when he dropped some vermicelli into the boiling water.

"Fixing me some?"

"Did you not eat?" he asked.

"That's irrelevant and immaterial and something else."

"Yes, I am."

"Even though I've already eaten?"

"Yes."

"This is love isn't it?" It didn't seem to bother her that he didn't answer. "So what's up?"

"Jennifer Bailey's niece is missing."

"Jasmine?"

"No, Jasmine's sister, Lianna."

"What do you think?"

"Don't know what to think. Driving home, I kept thinking that the police have a much better shot. But I'll look it over. Her boyfriend is upset. On the other hand, Lieutenant Swann has his eyes on the guy. Fight, breakup. Baby. Doesn't look good, she completely disappears right after all that."

28

Maureen opened a bottle of white wine. Shanahan opened a beer, dripped an ounce into the garlic butter sauce. Salt, pepper, and a little basil. That was it. They sat outside, looking at the stars. The full moon augmented the dim light coming from the kitchen window.

"Isn't this romantic?" Maureen said.

"She didn't tell anyone she was going, let alone where she was going."

"You know where I'd go when I leave you, which could be as early as after I finish the pasta?"

"I have no idea."

"You don't think I'd leave?"

"Sure. Probably for a restaurant owner."

"Close. I'd go to Italy. And I'd eat my way from Sicily to Tuscany." She sipped her wine. "Could we go to Italy?"

Her voice had changed. The last question was serious.

"Yes."

"You mean it?"

"I do."

Cross drove to the nearest National City Bank and deposited the check Channing's wife gave him as a retainer. He finished his report. It included an admission that he'd been caught out early in the final day's investigation. He prepared the invoice, praying that someone would pay it. The amount Mrs. Channing owed reflected six days' work, minus the advance. He felt it fair not to bill for the seventh day when his sleuthing talents were brought to an abrupt and embarrassing end. He would deliver the bill and the report in the morning.

He drove downtown to Amici's for spaghetti and Sangiovese, not minding that he could have found some fine Italian closer to home. He liked the lack of meticulousness in the restaurant's interior and the informality of the service. It was charming in its way, homey. He could relax. He could begin worrying about how to make ends meet tomorrow. Tonight was a holiday.

He slept a dreamless sleep and awoke the next morning having barely disturbed the covers of his bed.

In the morning he drove by Channing's security firm. The van was there. Cross proceeded to Channing's house, where he would present the report and the invoice. She was there. Her old Pontiac Firebird sat in the drive. But she wouldn't answer the door. He considered just leaving it, but thought better of it. He needed to see her personally. Channing had already gotten to her. He felt a wave of pity come over him. He hoped Channing wouldn't take it out on the little woman, literally the little woman. Cross thought about calling the police, but what could he tell them.

The call from Jennifer Bailey came a little after ten. Maureen had already left for some special showing of a home for her and dozens of other real estate agents. Shanahan spent the morning piddling about the house, cleaning Einstein's litter box, calling the pharmacy to renew his prescription for blood pressure medicine. Lost in his own world, the ring of the telephone surprised him. So did the news. It was good news, but it didn't make sense.

"I talked with Lieutenant Swann," Jennifer said after brief pleasantries. "Lianna boarded a plane for San Francisco yesterday afternoon. Her car was found at the airport. The ticket was charged to her American Express card."

There was a long pause.

"I don't know what to say."

"Yes, you do," she said, acknowledging that she too had some doubts.

"She's been gone three days, but she just got on a flight yesterday."

The sunlight in the window was suddenly absorbed in shadow.

"Yes," Jennifer said, "I thought about that. But who knows if we are privy to all that goes on in her life?"

"She left her car in paid airport parking?"

"I guess," Jennifer Bailey said with less certainty.

"You know something?"

"No. Just that she's an unpredictable girl . . . woman, I suppose . . . and this isn't exactly out of character for her. And I've seen it happen." She took a breath. "One day when I was a child, my father came home from work early. He took a bath, put on a clean shirt and then put on his best suit. I can remember looking out of the window as he walked away, right down the middle of Indiana Avenue. Not a care in the world. He never came back."

"You think she could do that?"

"I don't think my mother thought her husband could do that."

"Have you talked to Todd?"

"Yes. He seemed relieved and upset," she said. "Send the bill to me, Mr. Shanahan. He has enough on his mind."

"Nothing to send," Shanahan said. "I didn't really do much. Just some preliminary questions. I'm not sure I actually agreed to take the case."

Shanahan felt relieved too. Not just because it appeared she might be alive, but because he really thought the police would do a much more effective job of finding her. And they were, weren't they?

Shanahan wasn't all that keen on working anyway. He was retired. He and Maureen were getting by. He had his Army retirement, social security. She was doing all right in the real estate business and doing more all right all the time. Shanahan poured a cup of coffee and went outside to see a monstrous purplish-gray cloud nearly finish its journey across the sun. He picked up the bright-green tennis ball and tossed it straight up, high in the air. Casey moved quickly under it. The speckled hound knew to let it bounce and he caught it on the second descent.

He brought it back to Shanahan, then moved to the edge of the small lawn. Shanahan tossed it like a grounder to the short baseman. Casey dodged one way, the ball bounced the other. It didn't matter: Casey corrected his move, old bones and muscles be damned, and caught it.

31

The cloud cleared the sun.

"You going to be all right if we wander off to Italy?"

Over the next few days, Maureen scoured Fodor's *Italy* and printed out reams of paper from her Google searches. She talked him to sleep with debates about where they should go. Florence. Milan. Rome. Venice. The Amalfi Coast. They couldn't do it all, could they?

Shanahan, who thought it might be a nice thing for Maureen, was beginning to enjoy the prospect himself. He'd seen a bit of Europe while he was in the military. Would be nice to see it in a more leisurely, more civilized way. The last time they vacationed together it was in Hawaii. It was cut short. They owed themselves a relaxing time in the sun, he thought.

Cross cursed. His attempt to get cash from the cash machine failed. His chat with the teller inside revealed Channing had managed to stop the first check before it cleared the bank. This meant that the Channings had no intention of paying any of it.

Cross was out several hundred bucks. What made it worse was that it was his own stupidity that he was scammed out of the original retainer. That was his fault. Dumb, dumb, dumb, he thought. What could he do to Channing? He wanted to hurt him in some way. Cross knew better; but he had revenge on his mind. Channing would pay. He'd pay what he owed. And he'd pay for the time it took Cross to collect it. And he'd pay for—what was it they called it—mental anguish. Cross smiled. Who was he fooling?

Five

Shanahan, though he felt relieved to be off the case, couldn't control the unease that crept back into his psyche. He just didn't buy this sudden trip to San Francisco, but he wasn't sure what he could do about it. He was puzzling his dilemma when the phone rang. It was Todd Evans.

"I know people think Lianna went to San Francisco," he said. "Maybe she did. Maybe she just wanted out . . . of everything, everyone." There was silence.

Shanahan didn't know what to say. Todd was leading up to something, something Shanahan was sure he wouldn't like.

Then finally, he said, "I want you to go out there and find her."

"Hey Todd, listen—"

"I'll pay. I have the money."

"You know how big San Francisco is? She might not even be there. She might have gone to one of the cities in the Bay Area. There are dozens of San Mateos, San Raphaels, San Anselmos, San Whatevers, not to mention the El Cities and the La Cities. There's millions and millions of people there."

"I need to know," Todd said.

"Two things. One, if you insist on finding her, it would be best to hire someone out there. Two, ask yourself if you really want to find someone who has gone to all of this trouble not to be found?"

"I don't think she's there," Todd said.

"Just a moment ago you wanted me to go to San Francisco and find her."

"No one, not the police certainly, will look for someone they don't believe to be missing."

Now Shanahan got it, but it didn't help. It would be pretty hard to prove a negative. Even so, it wasn't at all practical for Shanahan to do it.

"If you get someone out there you won't have all the travel expenses to pay for. I'd have a hell of a time knowing where to start in a city I know nothing about."

"Please," Todd said. "How can I trust someone at a distance? We could go out there together. I can do the legwork. Surely, there's some way to track her down?"

"But you don't believe she's there?"

"It's complicated," he said.

Shanahan thought there might be some things he could do. If she'd rented a place somewhere, she'd probably have had to set up utility accounts. Used to be you could check out phone numbers. Now, with cell phones, it was pretty anonymous. Maybe there was a way to track anything she put on her charge cards.

"Let me do a few things from here and we'll see how it works out."

He hadn't agreed to take the case. He'd just agreed to look into it a little further. It was senseless for him to go to San Francisco. The fact was he liked the kid, felt sorry for him. There was also something nagging at Shanahan. He didn't think she'd gone anywhere either. She hadn't packed. Anything.

The Palace of Gold had a smattering of cars in the parking lot a little after 4 P.M. It opened at three thirty. Inside there were just two guys. The girls must have parked their cars in front to indicate the place was busier than it was. The place was spotless. Not easy to do, when every surface, covered in either brass or mirror, required a lot of maintenance to keep the shine.

A small blonde was on stage. Neither she nor the two guys in the audience seemed particularly interested.

Cross went to the bar. Instead of the young guy from last night, it was an older man, short-cropped hair, an honorable admission he was in a losing battle to cover his balding scalp. He wore an earring in the right ear and a tattoo on his neck. "I was in here a couple of days ago," Cross said. "There was this long-legged black girl with platinum hair. Lots of feathers. Is she working today?"

"Nope," the guy said.

"When will she be back?"

"Twelfth of never," the bartender said, without looking at Cross. "Or maybe February 31st, I'm not sure."

"She move to another club?"

Not getting a drink order, the bartender had already moved to the back bar to polish and stack some glasses.

"I need to talk to her," Cross said.

"I'm oh-so sorry fella. Love's a bitch. You might try Dear Abbey."

"Was she fired?" Cross persisted.

Frustrated, the bartender came over, took a deep breath. "If I tell you what I know, would you go away?"

"I won't even say 'goodbye.'"

"She was supposed to be in for a noon show yesterday. Special party. Didn't make it. Didn't make it last night. Now, that is absolutely all I know."

"Doesn't it seem strange someone would quit in May just when all the horny tourists come to town?"

The bartender leaned across the bar, eyeball to eyeball with Cross. He didn't blink and his breath smelled of tobacco. Cross gave in. He backed away, tossed his business card on the bar, and headed for the door.

"If you hear from her, have her call me," Cross said. "I'll make it worth your while."

He should have asked for the owner, to check out whether or not Channing had business with the club or just with one of the girls. He'd try again tomorrow. Also, he'd call around, see if this platinum-haired exotic dancer moved to another club. With the Indianapolis 500 Race only weeks away, this was the time the girls would make the most money. They would want to be in Indy. In fact, girls from other cities would migrate here to take advantage of thousands of sex-starved, away-from-home, fun-loving race fans from around the world. Didn't make sense for her to just pack up and leave.

Maureen had learned to google. She was more than a little proficient on her own personal computer. She not only did house searches, but also had become a restaurant scout and, more recently, their own personal travel agent.

Shanahan took advantage of her skills, asking her to run Lianna Bailey. Nothing. He asked her to find out the utility companies serving San Francisco and the Bay Area. The biggest was Pacific Gas and Electric Company.

"Hello," Maureen said into the telephone. "Customer service, please."

After an inordinate amount of time and number of transfers, she found someone willing to listen.

"I'm sorry," Maureen said, "this is Lianna Bailey and I need to know if my electricity is turned on?" Quiet. "I just moved. I can drive to where I live, but I didn't write down the address." She looked at Shanahan, giving him the "I screwed up" look. "No, no," Maureen responded to a new question. "Can't you just look it up by name?" Maureen listened. "Just a yes or no, I don't need any personal information. I know my personal information. I'm about to stop at the supermarket and pick up tons of groceries. I need to know if my refrigerator works." She looked at Shanahan. "Lianna Bailey." She spelled it for them as Shanahan spelled it out for her. "Oh." Quiet. "OK." Quiet. "Yes, well I guess it isn't on yet. Thank you for all your trouble." She looked up at Shanahan. "They don't have any Lianna Baileys."

She could be staying in a hotel, Shanahan thought. He'd try to call Swann tomorrow morning. See if there was any way they could track down any new credit card transactions. He'd also try to find out about ATM transactions.

Shanahan called Mary Beth Schmidt, Lianna's close friend

and coworker. Mary Beth agreed to meet him at the Chatterbox on Massachusetts Avenue, near where Lianna lived, and apparently near Mary Beth too. He'd meet her at five thirty. He also tried to reach Bradley Gray Pedersen, CEO of Noah Rose & Company, and Lianna's purported mentor through the corporate switchboard. He couldn't get close.

It might help to know the real reason Lianna wanted to escape. It might also help to know whether she had some special interest in San Francisco or perhaps a connection or two that Todd didn't know about. Best friends and mentors might be privy to that kind of information.

Maureen went along with Shanahan. Shanahan thought that Lianna's friend might feel more comfortable having another woman around rather than just the harsh and no doubt strange presence of some old geezer asking what could be embarrassing questions. After the meeting, Shanahan figured, maybe he and Maureen would find a nice little restaurant downtown on the Avenue. There were a couple of new places and Maureen deserved something more than another night of pasta and baseball. Then again, she didn't seem to mind pasta and baseball.

The Chatterbox was a great little bar, narrow, slightly rundown. It was the place musicians came to after their performances elsewhere were over.

Mary Beth was blond, well dressed, pretty in an athletic sort of way. Clear blue eyes, soft spoken, sincere in tone without coming off as an ingenue. But there was something distant about her. If she warmed to anyone, it was to Maureen, but it was only because she didn't fix her gaze on Maureen with the same blank look she gave Shanahan, as if he were a suspect in a peeping Tom case.

About Lianna's sudden and unexpected departure Mary Beth seemed as perplexed as everyone else. Mary Beth couldn't recollect that a trip to San Francisco was on any of Lianna's wish lists. As far as Mary Beth knew, Lianna had no friends in the City by the Bay.

"Paris, Barcelona, Rome," Mary Beth said. "She wasn't all that taken with American cities. I think she'd been everywhere."

"What about Asian cities or Australia?" Shanahan asked, thinking perhaps a trip to San Francisco was just a stop on her way west.

"No. Definitely Europe."

Shanahan pressed for more information about Lianna's state of mind, her relationship with Todd, and the possibility she was having an affair.

"Stable," she replied to the first question. "Touch and go," was the answer to the second question. "She was a very private person," was the answer to the third. The description Mary Beth painted verified what Shanahan had learned from Jennifer Bailey and from Todd Evans. Ambitious, smart. She knew what she wanted and was quite able to achieve it.

Unfortunately, none of what she said cast any light on the shadows of Lianna's life. Nothing new or insightful. The investigation without direction would continue that way.

Shanahan and Maureen dined much more contemporarily than they imagined. Strangely shaped chairs gave the dining area an inter-galactic Alice in Wonderland look. The food was a little pricey. All in all, it was pleasant.

"What do you think of Mary Beth?" Shanahan asked.

"She didn't know much about her best friend," Maureen said. "Lianna was pregnant, having trouble in her relationship, a rising star at the company, and what did she know? Lianna loved Europe. She has to know more than that."

Maureen was happy. Shanahan gave in and the two shared a bottle of Zinfandel. He was beginning to like wine. Especially with food. Perhaps an old dog can . . . In any event, Shanahan had made the effort and he wouldn't have to go out to dinner for a week or two.

They were home by eight thirty. The answering machine blinked.

"Hey, Shanahan," said Howie Cross. "Into drugs big time, eh? Let me know what you're up to. Just remember if this Pedersen character offers you some, just say no."

Shanahan, who had worked on a few cases and once saved the younger detective's life, had asked Cross to see if some of his old friends at IPD could get Bradley Gray Pedersen's unlisted home phone. He also provided the CEO's address. A phone call to the Pedersen household didn't get Shanahan any further than his earlier call to corporate headquarters. Saying that he was calling in reference to Lianna Bailey did him no good. Whoever it was on the other end of the line wasn't high enough on the chain of authority to let anyone in she didn't know; though she was willing to take a message. When Shanahan insisted, she became apologetic.

"I'm very sorry. Mr. Pedersen is holding a fundraiser tonight. He's very busy. I'm not sure he'd take a call from the White House."

Shanahan didn't know what kind of fundraiser it was, but he was willing to chip in a couple of bucks if that would get him in the front door. Then again the couple of bucks he was prepared to give wouldn't get him through the front door. Or the back door, for that matter. Might not even be able to get his antique Chevy Malibu into a driveway full of BMWs, Mercedeses, and Lincolns. Someone of Pedersen's stature would have some serious security for an event in his home. Delivery. He could pull the old Indianapolis Power & Light routine. Gas leak. Nope. Even if Harry's van worked, it was now too dilapidated to convince anyone that it was in the service of the Power Company.

He'd think of something.

He asked Maureen to call the private number again, suggesting she was a reporter for a local network affiliate. "What's the fundraiser for?" she asked.

"Political," the woman said. "Our senior senator."

The person who answered the phone apologized, saying that the evening wasn't open to the media. Just a few friends, some local political and social organizations.

Maureen said that she understood and said goodbye.

"Maybe you could go as an organization. The Gray Panthers or something," Maureen said.

"I'm not feeling particularly pantherish."

"How about . . . the gray foxes."

"I'm not foxy either."

"Gray squirrels?" She smiled.

"Now you have it," Shanahan said. "Dealing with nuts at all levels."

When she wanted to go along and he told her that she wasn't old enough, she protested. "But I could be your caretaker. Wheel you in."

"Oh," Shanahan said. "That's an excellent idea. You're brilliant!"

Perhaps it was taking advantage of one's goodwill, but most people have difficulty turning away someone in a wheelchair. Even more to the point, what would it look like for a gathering of the city fathers—and the city was still run by fathers rather than mothers—to have it known they ejected a senior?

Six

Cross didn't want to visit every strip joint in Indianapolis. There were a number of them—perhaps some new ones he didn't even know about. So he sat down at the little kitchen table with the *Yellow Pages*, skipping those places he knew to be too sleazy for the talent he saw on stage. This time of night would be the best time to call the clubs—between the happy-hour crowd and the late-night audience.

His line was the same. "Sorry to bother you, but this dancer I really like just left the Palace of Gold and I was hoping to see her again before I leave for Cleveland." He described the long-legged dancer with the blond wig.

Impatient, he got up, paced. Finally, while he waited through interminable rings for someone to pick up the phone, he pulled a beer from the refrigerator. He hung up.

Standing at the kitchen counter, sipping the cool liquid, listening to "Black Magic Woman," he dialed another number, was put on hold. His character was one of those sad souls who developed a crush on a fantasy. A lonely guy who imagined that one of the dancers actually found him desirable. There were plenty of those. Surprisingly, for the most part, the bartenders and managers responded with some level of compassion. They made an attempt to be helpful, but in the end the answer was always disappointing. As far as Cross could tell, the platinum-haired, long-legged beauty hadn't hired on locally.

He could talk to the other dancers. That was about his only chance. He'd try tomorrow afternoon, before the shows started. That way he wouldn't spend hours just talking to a couple of dancers and tipping for information.

In the interim, he seethed. Cross was still smarting from the stop payments on the check Channing's wife gave him. He had been punked by the big, dumb ex-cop from Cincinnati.

Shanahan couldn't figure out where to get a wheelchair at this time of night; but he did have a cane stashed away somewhere. He found a pair of pants that were in decent shape and appropriately a little too big for him. He found a shirt that he had bought but never wore with a tie because the neck was one size too large. Through clothing, posture, and gait, Shanahan was able to age himself by at least a decade.

Maureen drove. The night was warm; but not humid. The stars were visible. A not quite half moon illuminated even the darker corners of the big lawns as they approached the high-rent district. No longer the only posh area in the city, Meridian Street nonetheless remained the oldest posh area.

A few streets beyond the Governor's mansion, was the Pedersen home. Police had allowed parking all along the major north-south artery in order to accommodate the crowd.

The two of them parked several blocks away. Shanahan had to poke along the sidewalk as if he were one of the frail elderly. A uniformed guard didn't stop them as they walked up the drive toward the front door of a mammoth Tudor brick home, lights blazing inside.

"I didn't know the Tudors came through Indianapolis," Maureen said, smiling.

"A realtor joke?"

"Yes, sorry."

A black man as big as a Colt's linebacker, who wore a black suit and crisp white shirt and a headphone, politely stopped them at the door.

"Your invitation, please?" he asked graciously.

"You've got it, of course, Florence," Shanahan said.

"Oh dear, no," Maureen said, overacting. Maureen wasn't a convincing ingenue. "I thought you had it."

"Just your name," the man said. "It's all right."

42

"Dietrich Shanahan," he said, giving his real name in the event credentials would be required.

The man pulled a small phone from his jacket pocket. He cupped his hand, so no one could hear what he was saying. After he spoke, he waited. Concern soon lined his face. Then pain, as he spoke to Shanahan.

"I'm terribly sorry. We don't have you down."

"Mr. Shanahan is a member of the American Association of Retired Persons," Maureen said. "We're very supportive of the Senator. Oh, dear. What will they say at the office if they won't let us in?"

The man at the door swallowed another attempt at a smile. "Let me check again."

It was fun being old, Shanahan thought. He should have tried this little trick earlier. It was just a shame that he didn't have to use make-up to pull it off.

Others came and went as Shanahan and Maureen waited. Finally, a young man in a blue striped shirt and bow tie came up to them.

"Mr. Shanahan, ma'am," he said to them, almost but not quite bowing. "We're so sorry there's been a mix up with the invitations and the Senator is very happy you're here. I'm sure he'll want to talk to you before the evening's over."

He led them into the main living area, which was crowded with well-dressed Republicans and those without party affiliation who didn't care who was Senator as long as they could buy some influence. Certainly the CEO of one of the largest drug companies in the world would want one of the country's most powerful senators to understand the "difficult" plight of the pharmaceutical industry.

Shanahan wasn't sure what plight that would be.

Maureen looked around in awe or hunger; it was difficult for Shanahan to tell. Maybe she was just casing the place. What a prize sale this would be for a real estate agent. He had, however, imagined a more ostentatious display of wealth. Instead, he found quiet good taste. He could live there, if he could stretch his social security check and his meager earnings as an investigator that far.

Wine was brought and both of them plucked a glass of red from the tray. Maureen seemed happy. Shanahan hoped she'd remember not to be too vivacious. Caregivers weren't supposed to have sex appeal. As for Shanahan, he had to remember to be old and fragile, a role he found increasingly and depressingly easy to play.

"Florence?" Maureen asked when she could speak to him with some privacy. "Why not Miss Nightingale?"

"I didn't want to overdo it," Shanahan said.

Shanahan scanned the room to see if he could locate Pedersen and to make sure there was no one there who could blow his cover. Not likely in this crowd, he thought. He was mistaken. He didn't find Pedersen. But there was Mary Beth Schmidt, in a black dress, blond hair on top of her head, sluicing through the crowd. He nudged Maureen and whispered his dilemma. She nodded toward the doors at the opposite end of the room. There was more party outside. They went around the edge of the crowd to shield themselves from view.

"Is she that high in the company?" Maureen whispered.

"I didn't think so," Shanahan said. "Hired help."

"She was dressed pretty well for an employee on overtime. And she walked as if she owned the joint."

"Let's check her out again. Maybe she's just eye candy," he said.

Maureen gave him a dirty look. "Watch your sweets, kiddo."

As it turned out, the inside population was only the tip of the iceberg. Outside *was* the party. The huge stone patio was not enough to contain the folks. They spilled out on the soft green lawn, subtly lit by embedded lights. A man sat on a bench under a lamp pole that emanated a soft salmon-colored light. He played classical guitar.

Shanahan saw the silver-haired senator, a man who was re-elected each year by a landslide with minimal need for electioneering funds. Nonetheless the vested interests were here, backing a sure thing. The Senator, loved by his fellow Hoosiers, nonetheless spent most of his time on a farm in

Virginia when he wasn't in DC. Nobody seemed to care that Indiana's senators preferred to live elsewhere.

Shanahan also spotted Pedersen. He was in a group adjacent to the Senator's little gathering. Shanahan ambled as feebly as he could toward the CEO. Shanahan rarely felt stage fright in these kinds of situations. But this wasn't his usual crowd. This was the rich and powerful. A guy could pawn the collected watches of the attendees and retire half the national debt.

Pedersen talked with five others, all men, except for the host's wife Lauren, whom Shanahan recognized from the newspapers.

Pedersen was the first to notice the aging interloper. He graciously stopped talking and focused everyone's attention on Shanahan. The little group parted, allowing Shanahan to enter. Pedersen, a man in his early sixties but looking years younger, fit, extremely tanned and with the whitest teeth the detective had ever seen, smiled at Shanahan with the same kind of warmth one reserves for puppies. A kindly, curious condescension. The pleasure that Shanahan felt when the guards showed deference was replaced by an intense displeasure. He didn't like the notion that someone might consider him "cute."

"Could we talk in private?" Shanahan asked directly of Pedersen.

Pedersen looked at the others, shrugged a "why-not" with an even broader grin. Oh, he thinks the puppy wants to play, Shanahan thought. The two of them stepped into the shadows. Shanahan found it hard to hide his resentment.

"What can I do for you?" Pedersen asked.

"I want you to tell me what you know about Lianna Bailey's disappearance."

The kindness in Pedersen's eyes gave way to anger. He controlled his voice better than he controlled his eyes. His anger was reduced to caution as he spoke.

"I'm really sorry. Who are you exactly?"

"My name is Dietrich Shanahan. I am a private investigator looking into the disappearance of Lianna Bailey."

Pedersen's face was granite. "I believe that at the moment the state's attorney general, as well as Lianna's loved ones, would also appreciate your cooperation." Shanahan played the card. He hoped he hadn't presumed too much.

"I don't know anything more than what everyone else seems to know," Pedersen said with forced civility. "That is that she didn't show up for work on Monday morning. We're all deeply concerned, and I would love to help you if I could. My heart goes out to the family during these trying times." This was the polished politically savvy statement CEOs, like senators, learn how to do faced with something unpleasant.

"I'm not a reporter, Mr. Pedersen. I'm a detective."

Pedersen squinted. It was vintage Clint Eastwood.

"Was she unhappy at work?" Shanahan continued.

"Not to my knowledge." Pedersen was holding his anger in, though the emotion seemed to be struggling to get out anyway. His head shook in quick, light tremors.

"Was she under any other kind of pressure you were aware of?" Shanahan asked.

"No," he provided an insincere smile. Anger began to seep into his voice. "I'm afraid I can't help you."

"But you were very close. You were described as her mentor."

"While I appreciate the gravity of the situation, now isn't the time or the place to conduct this kind of business. Maybe we can meet under more conducive circumstances—though again, there's nothing much I can tell you. So, if you'll excuse me."

"Was she having an affair with anyone?" Shanahan asked to the man's back.

Pedersen didn't answer, or turn.

With his voice slightly raised, Shanahan pressed ahead. "Were the two of you romantically involved?"

Now Pedersen turned on a dime. He came back to Shanahan as if he were going to strike him.

"You had to have entered here under false pretenses, Mr. whoever in the hell you are."

"Shanahan. I told the truth at the door. I told them I was a member of AARP." Shanahan returned the insincere smile. "I am."

"Don't press your luck." In the morning, I'm calling the police and filing a complaint. Any additional interference from you will be dealt with in ways you really don't want to understand. Have I made myself clear?"

"You speak clearly, Mr. Pedersen. I'm surprised you need the reassurance."

Pedersen looked around, no doubt trying to flag down security. Shanahan retrieved Maureen and together they moved back inside and toward the door.

"Surely, they won't beat up an old man with a cane," Maureen said, grinning as they emerged in front, heading for the sidewalk.

"Not in brightly lit places, with a US senator around, they won't."

When Cross crawled in bed, his brain was still on fire. He was rabid with notions of revenge. He knew his feelings were childish. He couldn't help but think about ordering pizzas from every pizza dealer in town and have them delivered to the Channings. The problem was it would be the poor pizza guys who would suffer. Channing would never pay up. He thought about calling a tow company, telling them to pick up Channing's van. But he wouldn't wish Channing on anyone. He hated it. Channing was winning. He had Cross sputtering. A bottle of Chianti kindly blurred the edges. Even so, it was almost dawn before his brain cooled down enough for him to drift off into an uneasy sleep.

Seven

If Shanahan's morning was any indication, this wasn't going to be a good day. He cut himself shaving, spilled a cup of coffee while trying to keep Einstein away from Maureen's breakfast, and he glanced unhappily out of the living room window to see Lieutenant Max Rafferty get out of a big black Chevy Caprice,

The plump, bearded, and sartorially splendiferous policeman had, over recent years, become the face of the Indianapolis Police Department. His verbal command of ambiguity and his instincts for self-preservation translated well in his role as the unofficial but quite effective PR cop. He was the perfect official to schmooze the media, soften hostile commissions, and deliver a positive twist to the image of the police in classrooms of the third-graders. In his defense, Rafferty was also the cop to call when a criminal was holding hostages or a depressed soul was ready to jump. In another life, Shanahan thought, maybe Rafferty could have been a horse whisperer, coaxing, convincing, manipulating. In this life he was the Police Department's fixer.

The Rafferty Shanahan knew was unpredictable. Whenever he saw the increasingly corpulent cop, Shanahan never knew whether he was going to get a pat on the back or a knock on the head. Rafferty was more than willing to cross the line if it was in his best interest and knew he wouldn't get caught.

He was something of a legend in the force. The stereotype suggested that cops liked football, doritos and fast cars. Rafferty was addicted to expensive restaurants, aged Scotch and expensive clothes. When asked to explain how he could afford Burberry on a cop's salary, Rafferty would say, "I have no other vices. This is what I live for."

He had other vices. He just didn't have to pay for them.

Now he sat in Shanahan's living room, a trip prompted by a Pedersen complaint.

"I got lots of news for you today," Rafferty said, making himself comfortable. He seemed to be enjoying himself.

"One is under the headline 'Powerful Pharmaceutical CEO pissed at lowly P.I.,'" Shanahan said.

"The rich are different from you and me," Rafferty said.

"Me anyway," Shanahan said.

"There are a couple of dozen folks in this city, just like any other city, you don't fuck with. Bradley Gray Pedersen is one of them."

"And you are here to do what?"

"Scare the hell out of you and go back and tell the man that you've been properly reamed and that you regret ever stepping foot on his property or interfering with his life in any way." Rafferty smiled.

"How do you propose to do it?"

"What, scare the hell out of you? I just did." He smiled again. He was having fun. "I'm not looking to do any damage here. You just need to stay out of Pedersen's way."

Maureen came into the room, saw Rafferty and went back to the kitchen. Her experience with Rafferty went way back and it wasn't pleasant. Casey, who uncharacteristically failed to welcome the guest, remained on alert.

"Nice to see you," Rafferty called out to the empty doorway.

"The problem is that with the investigation," Shanahan said, trying to stay civil, "I may need to know more from Mr. Pedersen. He was close to Lianna."

"You really don't have a problem."

"No?"

"No. Because you don't have a case."

"Lianna's been found?"

"No. Lianna's an active case. No private investigators allowed."

"Last I heard she is a missing person. We're not banned from looking for missing people."

"The last you heard was simply the last you heard."

"I'm not sure I'm hearing anything different from you."

"See, it's now a murder investigation."

"No body, right?"

"Don't need a body. It'd be nice to have a body, but don't need a body." Rafferty was enjoying himself. Shanahan thought he must not have a lot to do to spend so much time trying to entertain. Then again, he was only entertaining himself.

"You tell jokes in front of a mirror at home?"

"I'm telling you this because . . . well, Hell, I'm telling you this because if I didn't Swann probably would. Seems as if your boy Todd took out a one million dollar insurance policy on Lianna less than a month before her disappearance." Rafferty paused for effect. "And according to a witness, and very contradictory to Todd's statement, it was Todd who didn't want the baby."

Shanahan hoped his face didn't show surprise. But Rafferty knew.

"Didn't know that, did you?" Rafferty asked with the glee of a nine-year-old.

It was clear Rafferty had been briefed thoroughly. The reason was clear as well. Once the newspapers got hold of the murder angle, this already front-page story could turn into another media obsession. He wouldn't be surprised to see Peter Jennings lead off the ABC evening news with the arrest.

"Have you charged him with the murder?"

"At the moment, he's a 'person of interest.'"

"Officially a person of interest."

Rafferty's face said it. He knew what Shanahan was thinking.

"You better think long and hard about this. Your old pal Jennifer Bailey no longer looks at Lianna's boyfriend with favor. No one on the force is gonna be happy if you go litter the trail with your ancient antics. The public is not going to think much of you either. Lianna was with child. A mother. Boyfriend offs her because he doesn't want the responsibility for the child, but does want the money. Nobody is going to like anybody they think is on his side."

"Everybody is entitled to a defense, Rafferty. Even you."

"In a perfect world, I suppose."

"You've got him convicted already."

Rafferty nodded. "It's in the bag. Just a matter of time. Save yourself some agony and read about it in the newspapers." Rafferty got up, pulled some folded papers from his suit jacket. "By the way, this is a restraining order. You get too close to Pedersen you go to jail." Rafferty smiled the gotcha smile. "You shouldn't play rough with the big boys."

Rafferty went to the door. He stopped as if he were going to say something else, then changed his mind. Then changed it again. "Say hi to your woman." It was hard to tell whether or not he meant that in a kindly way. For all his slick diplomacy in police politics, he didn't have a lot of what Maureen would call interpersonal skills.

"Say hi to the big boys," Shanahan said.

"Hey, with them, I only speak when I'm spoken to. I learned my place a long time ago. And here you are—in God's waiting room—and you still haven't figured that out."

"Well, that was a pleasant way to start the day," Maureen said, coming into the living room.

"Yes, nice to be told you are old and bumbling by a happy face." Shanahan went to the kitchen for more coffee. "I also received my first restraining order."

"I've thought about it myself a few times," she said, following him.

"They told me that I couldn't help young Todd at the very time they are going to come down hard on him."

"What do you think?"

"Somebody said that it was Todd who didn't want the kid."

"Who said that?"

"Don't know. They didn't say. But somebody's lying." Now

what would he do? No sooner had he questioned himself and then Maureen, Jennifer Bailey called.

In the least threatening way possible, she threatened him, told him he must not look into the disappearance any further. He should quit Todd Evans.

"Who or what caused this sudden guilty verdict?"

"We need to keep some things quiet now," she said, trying to say it diplomatically, trying also to induce Shanahan to a sympathetic response. "I'm asking you as a friend—"

He interrupted. He never interrupted her.

"If, as you told me earlier, you think I am honest, someone with principle, why are you worried?"

"I'm not worried."

"What do you have to fear?"

"I'm sorry," she said, her tone turning frigid, "you'll just have to do what you have to do, I suppose; but as I understand the law with regard to homicide investigations, you are no longer permitted to investigate."

"Unless his lawyer hires me to do so," he said.

She was quiet.

He liked her, respected her, but he didn't like anyone pushing him around. He could see the forces bearing down on Todd as well. Bailey was using her influence to motivate the police, and her friendship to make Shanahan behave. And there was Pedersen using his influence to keep himself from answering questions the police weren't about to ask one of the city's muckety mucks.

"You afraid of Pedersen too?"

She didn't answer.

"Maybe Todd is guilty," he continued, "but I don't like to see anybody ganged up on."

He heard the phone click. She was always the kind to save her arguments for the courtroom.

Shanahan searched through his wallet for the piece of paper that contained Todd's phone number.

Todd picked up right away.

"The police are here. They're boxing up all our papers, hauled out both our computers. They're searching through everything. You know they took our vacuum cleaner, our mops and sponges. Why are they taking the vacuum cleaner?"

"Have you talked to them?" Shanahan asked. He knew why they took the cleaning equipment, but he didn't want to tell Todd just yet.

"They won't talk to me. They just glare at me whenever I say anything," Todd said. His voice showed stress, but it seemed strong enough.

"OK, if they ask who you talked to tell them it was me telling you that I was quitting the case," Shanahan said.

"What?"

"I'm telling you that right now. If they ask you, just tell them I'm off the case, OK?" He wished he could say more, but he couldn't take the chance.

"Yes," Todd said tentatively. Hurt possibly.

"Whatever you do, do not answer any questions. Find a lawyer. Have your lawyer call me. Do you know a lawyer?"

"Miss Bailey," he said.

"No. Find your own. I mean it."

"I know a tax lawyer," he said.

"Have that lawyer help you find a good criminal lawyer. Right away."

There were loud words in the background.

"Who is this?" came a strange, dark and angry voice.

"Who is this?" Shanahan asked as impolitely, though he knew who it was.

"We'll find you. Tracing this call is real easy," the voice said.

"This is Dietrich Shanahan, officer. I'm a private investigator who is doing exactly what Police Lieutenant Max Rafferty said, backing off the case since it is now a homicide investigation."

"Who said it was a homicide investigation?"

"It isn't?"

Quiet.

"You said your name was Shanahan?" He was no doubt writing it down in his little notebook.

"Dietrich Shanahan. What are you doing with the kid?"

"None of your business," the cop said.

"Who am I talking to?" Shanahan wanted to know in case something happened to Todd.

"I'll ask the questions, pal."

"You'll play hell getting any more answers then."

Shanahan put the phone back in the cradle. He told Maureen he'd be gone for awhile. "You're on your own for lunch."

"I need your help," Shanahan told Cross, who sat in an old, overstuffed 1940s brown mohair sofa in his living room, once the garage of a chauffeur's quarters. Not counting a small kitchen and bath, there were only two other rooms. One was a smallish room just inside the door that once served as the chauffeur's studio. Someone, at some point, had added a small bedroom off the bath. The former garage was a couple of steps down and could easily have fit two cars. It had high ceilings and big Mediterranean arched doorways, now sliding doors that led out to a graveled patio with two pine trees.

Shanahan sat in an old English highback chair that even in the old detective's fashion-free mind, seemed mismatched to the sofa and to the rest of the room. But then nothing in the room seemed to go with anything else—and in an odd way everything seemed to work.

Noticing Shanahan looking around, Cross seemed to pick up on Shanahan's thoughts.

"Based on my success as a cop and private eye, I am seriously thinking about taking up interior design. Not that I'm gay," Cross said, smiling. "Though that too needs further thought. Based on my recent luck with women—lack of it, I mean—guys may be an option worth exploring."

"It sounds like you've thought this through," Shanahan said.

"Yes," he said as he sipped coffee, "but while I am wallowing in all these strange transitions in my life, I suppose I can still help you."

"I've got a restraining order preventing me from getting anywhere near Bradley Gray Pedersen or Noah Rose and Company."

"And this is a bad thing?" Cross said, grinning.

As Shanahan started to explain the Todd Evans case, he discovered he didn't have to explain very much. Cross had already read the morning newspaper. A front-page, top-of-the-fold story said the police were "acting as if it were a homicide investigation" rather than a simple disappearance. They also indicated, though did not name, that Lianna Bailey's fiancé was a "person of interest."

"I love that, 'person of interest,'" Cross said. "I wish I could be a person of interest, but I've said that already."

"Poor baby," Shanahan said.

"You think Mr. Pedersen is involved."

"Young Lianna was climbing up through the glass ceiling very quickly through the kindness of her boss."

"That's a big jump," Cross said.

"That's what got me into trouble. I jumped a little too quick. He was stonewalling me and I needed him to respond to something. Older mentor, young, ambitious assistant. I thought I'd get a rise."

"And indeed you did. He struck back right away and with force, I take it."

"He needs to be ruled in or out," Shanahan said.

"Especially in," Cross said.

Shanahan refused to admit it.

"Nature never made teeth that white," Shanahan said.

Half an hour later, the phone rang. It was Todd. After hello and before anything else, Shanahan stopped him.

"I don't like telephones." Shanahan figured the phone was bugged.

There was quiet.

"I need to see you. There is no one else I can turn to."

"Listen, we need to settle up the bill," Shanahan said, hoping that Todd could read between the lines. "Are you home?"

"Yes," Todd said. His voice was small.

"I'll meet you in front of your place. We'll go for a walk and I'll tell you what I learned before I quit the case. Just so you get your money's worth. It's not much."

Shanahan wanted to ask him many more questions.

"You hire a lawyer yet?"

"Don't know where to go."

"Maybe I connect you to one." Shanahan looked at his watch. "I'm coming over now. Twenty minutes, OK?"

"OK."

Eight

C ross spent the morning and early afternoon googling the drug company's CEO, Pedersen. Born in San Mateo, California, graduated with an MBA from Stanford in Palo Alto. On the boards of various San Francisco-based corporations. Married with three children, all old enough to be out on their own now. Ran the pharmaceutical company for less than five years, having sold his not-quite controlling interest in a biophysics company, headquartered in San Mateo. Active in the Republican Party, behind the scenes. He supported conservative think tanks—not the one with fundamentalist Christian bent, but ones that boasted a certain intellectual prowess.

It appeared from all the stories in various publications—from *Forbes* and *Fortune* to *Vanity Fair* and *Time*—that once he moved to Indianapolis, he began to support local causes. The museum. The Symphony. In business, it was another story. He retained his seats on various San Francisco boards; yet didn't add any local businesses to his résumé.

So, he was successful, respected, and charitable. He was, by all accounts, successful as a father and as a family man, having married once. The only blemish on the guy's report card might be no check in the box where they say "gets along well with others."

Without saying why, the stories implied he didn't leave Mason Life Systems willingly. He only left it richer and in demand. Noah Rose & Company—or Rose as it was called in the city—snatched him up quickly and the business publications heralded Pedersen as the perfect prescription for a bloated, sedentary company. With someone at the helm who

57

was young, energetic, and a little more future oriented, Rose's stocks ballooned long before performance showed the decision to hire Pedersen was a wise one.

Cross printed out some info on Mason Life Systems, including the names of the twenty-five members of the corporation's board of directors, their titles, and the companies they worked for.

He called Shanahan, caught him as he was leaving.

"You're not alone. The board of directors of Mason Life Systems didn't like Pedersen much either."

"Why?"

"Wouldn't say," Cross said. "It's all kind of mysterious. News releases suggested that Pedersen was pursuing personal interests and wanted to spend more time with his family."

"Not original, is it? What is Mason Life Systems?"

"Bioengineering," Cross said.

"And that means?"

"All sorts of things, changing the DNA of corn so that it doesn't reproduce."

"Why would someone want to do that?"

"So the farmers have to buy new seeds every planting season. It could also mean designer babies. You want your kid to be a boy with blue eyes, blond hair and a generous endowment, you check the boxes, put your order in. Then, there's the whole cloning thing. Maybe you'd like to create another Dietrich Shanahan."

"I can barely stand the current one. I think the twenty-first century left without me."

Todd Evans stood in front of the old brick building with huge factory windows. The Silk Factory had been turned into stylish condominiums. As Shanahan approached he caught the scent of alcohol layered with toothpaste. The boy had been drinking.

"You all right?" Shanahan asked.

"Yeah," he said unconvincingly. "You know what they had me do? They had me take off all my clothes and they inspected my body."

"Looking for scratches, bruises, thinking maybe you and Lianna had a fight that led . . ."

"I never ever touched her . . . that way."

"I know."

"How long is this going to go on?"

"It's just begun," Shanahan said. "How much have you had to drink?"

"The police took everything but the Scotch. It was unopened, I guess."

"Not a lot of Scotch drinkers on the force is my guess."

Rafferty apparently wasn't along for the search, Shanahan thought. That should have been obvious. Tossing Evans's place was actually police work.

"So, you are deserting me too?" Evans asked, much too sorrowfully for Shanahan's taste.

"Todd, don't start feeling sorry for yourself. Leave drinking and sorry to the Irish. It's where it belongs," Shanahan said, knowing whereof he spoke. "I can't legally work for you because this has become a homicide investigation. But I can work for a lawyer who represents you." Shanahan nodded for Todd to follow him as they went back to the retail section of the neighborhood.

As they walked, Shanahan told Todd Evans that a lawyer took on cases whether or not the suspect was guilty or innocent because that was their job. But that this wasn't necessarily Shanahan's approach. Shanahan said that if Todd was guilty of anything criminal, the young man would find hiring Shanahan a poor investment.

"I don't know what happened to Lianna," he said, still feeling sorry for someone. "I want all of this to end. I want her to come back and . . ." His words tailed off into nothing.

They stopped at a small Greek restaurant, Aesop's, for a bite of lunch. They sat, looked at the menus in tense silence. Shanahan waited until the waiter took the order before he spoke.

"You took out a policy on Lianna. Life insurance. Just a month or so ago."

"At her insistence," Todd said.

"You went along with it."

"Yes. We were going to buy a really nice home on the Northside. Helluva mortgage. We could only get the loan if we combined both our incomes. She was the beneficiary of my insurance and I was the beneficiary of hers. It was a safeguard for each other. It was good business."

"Word is—and I don't know just where that word came from—that you didn't want the baby. That you were angry about it."

"I was. At first. We had a plan. A financial plan. To buy a home, get our careers on track and then we would decide when it was the right time to have a child, children really. We wanted two, but not right away. This was a slip. I was upset. But within days I started thinking about what a child would mean, something that was part of her and part of me. Joined. Ours. I thought, especially as she started to distance herself, that this would be the one thing that would bind us together."

"Could she just go off to San Francisco?"

"Maybe. She had no family here. Neither do I. We shared that too. Her parents died. All she had was her sister and they didn't have a whole lot to do with each other. Lianna was into material things. Jasmine was a do-gooder. They were really just cool with each other. So, yes, she could go off if she really meant to leave me." He took a deep breath, thanked the waitress for bringing the salad. "On the other hand, it is very hard for me to believe she would leave Rose. That company, that job meant everything to her."

Shanahan left Todd on his own and walked the short distance to visit an attorney he knew. Once he was away from the old, restored neighborhood and back where business was business, he remembered the days when one of the buildings on this block of Pennsylvania Avenue housed a quiet little gay bar. The bar sat in the shadow of the keepers of morality. And it wasn't that long ago when conventional morality frowned on such things. Now, across from the once modern, junior skyscraper that was filled with city offices, including the mayor's and the municipal courtrooms, was a row of bars and bail bondsmen.

On the second floor of one of the old brick buildings— Mike's Express Bail occupied the ground level—was the law office of James Fenimore Kowalski. Somewhere in his mid to late sixties, Kowalski was a big man with big hair, big beard. There was very little black left in his hair and beard. It was mostly silver and swept wildly back. He had the look of Zeus, ready to throw a few thunderbolts if someone displeased him. He wore his suits loose, wrinkled, and black. Every time Shanahan saw him, Kowalski was wearing a white shirt with the top button not quite buttoned. Never a tie. It was as if he wore the suit to show his membership in the establishment and went tieless to show he wasn't about to obey all of their silly, little rules. He was a revolutionary. No one quite knew exactly what he was protesting—perhaps the rule of law, or the particular way the law ruled these days.

When he saw Shanahan he got up immediately, laughed heartily, and extended his hand.

"Well, I'll be. Never thought I'd see you again," Kowalski said.

"You thought I'd be dead by now?" Shanahan asked.

"No," he said matter-of-factly, "just never figured our paths would cross, you hanging around Jennifer Bailey and me hanging around the riffraff. So you decided to descend into the real world again." He sat back down. "Can I have my girl get you a beer?"

"No," Shanahan said, smiling, knowing full well Kowalski ran a one-person office in the one room they were in now.

"What's up?"

"I have a client for you."

"Who, what, when, where . . . don't be so mysterious."

"Murder maybe."

"You considering killing somebody?"

"Todd Evans."

"No shit," Kowalski said.

"You know already?" Shanahan asked but, giving it a second's thought, he understood.

"Lot of salivating going on around here. You think there'd be a battalion of Pavlov's ringing bells. All the deputy DAs want it or a piece of it; and all of the defense attorneys are sending their suits to the dry cleaners to make sure they're ready for CNN."

Kowalski paused, gave Shanahan the look. It said: "What are you doing to me?" He shook his head and grinned. "Now how is it you're in a position to offer me such a job?"

"You're not going to like everything you hear from now on," Shanahan said. He sat down on the rusty folding chair reserved for clients.

"Nice of you to warn me. Just let me know what you want me to do."

"Nothing."

"I've got that down pat."

"You'll get a modest retainer and then you'll get a monthly payment that you will give to me as your investigator."

"OK," he said, taking a deep breath as if the deal was now consummated.

"You really want a piece of this?"

"Yeah, you want me to be your beard. You want to investigate, but you can't as a private eye, except when you are working for an attorney. I can do that."

"And when the media descends upon your office?"

"How wonderful. I can entertain them for hours without saying anything," Kowalski said. "And that's good for business. And if I alienate the public, which I often do, when it comes time for a trial you can make a big deal about firing me."

Shanahan wasn't sure whether Kowalski was serious. Kowalski picked up on it.

"Damn, Shanahan, I like this. I really like it. Do you know how many overdressed, overpaid lawyers in their marble-floored offices will piss in their pants when they learn I'm defense counsel?"

"But . . ."

"I don't need to be the defense counsel," Kowalski said, answering Shanahan's unasked question. "I just need for them to believe it for a little while, just long enough to drive them crazy."

"Just curious," Shanahan said. "Why do you like to stir up trouble?"

"Because I'm disgusted with the human race," he said, lighting a cigar.

"All of us?"

"Pretty much. I remember when they tried to sell Skippy peanut butter on TV. There'd be this guy spreading the peanut butter on a piece of bread and he'd say something like, 'If you want rich and creamy peanut butter, try Skippy.'"

Kowalski looked at Shanahan to see if he'd made his point. He hadn't.

"OK," he continued. "You remember L.S.M.F.T.?"

"Lucky Strike means fine tobacco."

"Right. Simple, straightforward. They didn't know that smoking would kill you back then. Now they do. So what do they do? First, they try to get by with it. They lie to Congress, which didn't seem to matter to that august body of liars. But when they get found out, what do they do? They give money to smoking cessation programs. They set up websites to warn people, especially kids, that smoking that shit would kill you, so the public and the stock market will think they are reputable firms. That's what the left hand is doing. The right hand is plastering ads all over your local Seven Eleven encouraging people, especially kids, to smoke. This is all legal. Meanwhile, some poor pimple-faced teenager gets caught with a nickel bag of marijuana and he spends twenty years in prison."

Shanahan was glad he had the afternoon. "So you are saying what? Cigarettes are bad?"

"I'm saying the world is full of hypocritical bastards. I'm just one little grain of sand on the planet, but whenever I get a chance to piss off one of those hypocritical grains of sand on the planet, I do it." He opened the window to let the smoke out, then turned back to Shanahan, "So, when do I get to meet the little murderer?"

Cross waited patiently in his car in the parking lot of the Palace of Gold. The lot was empty and hot. No trees. No shade. He kept the engine running to take advantage of the air conditioning. He got there early so he could catch the girls before they went in for the late-afternoon show.

The van came into the lot, moved slowly. A man was driving. He eyed Cross but continued on, parking near the front door. Before disappearing around back, he again looked at Cross, who figured the guy would think it was just some impatient customer. A couple of cars entered the lot. One belonged to the bartender he talked to earlier. The other probably belonged to one of the dancers. He didn't want to engage the bartender, so Cross decided to wait until he could get one of the dancers alone. He began to feel like a leopard on the prowl. He hoped he wouldn't come across that way with the dancers.

Nearly thirty minutes passed before he saw a Nissan Altima pull in. It had the look of a rental car. A tall, slender woman wearing blue jeans and a T-shirt got out. She had opened the back door of her sedan and was gathering some clothes on hangers. He got out of the car and called out to her.

"Excuse me?" he shouted as he approached her. When she turned toward him, the look of surprise on her face suggested he had scared her. "I'm sorry," he said as he came closer.

"Howie?" she said. It wasn't fear, it was shock.

"Jesus," he said. "Margot."

"What are you doing here?" she asked.

She wasn't wearing makeup, her hair was longer, and she had changed the color from brunette to dishwater blond.

"I was about to ask you the same thing."

"Part of the circuit. You know Mardi Gras in New Orleans, the Derby in Louisville. Well, it's May. So it's Indianapolis. Started a couple of nights ago."

"I was here a couple of times, didn't see you."

"I don't work both shifts. And you? I thought you gave up on dancers."

"I did. I'm working," he said.

"Parking attendant?" she smiled. "Or maybe the new bouncer."

"Long story. Basically a no pay was connected somehow to one of the dancers here. I'd like to know how; but I can't seem to find her. I thought maybe one of the dancers knew more about her. She was here dancing a few days ago. Now she's gone."

"Which one?"

"Black girl, platinum wig, feathers."

"Norah."

"You know her?"

"Our paths crossed from time to time. Nice girl. She didn't like the work; but she liked the money and the stage."

"You're saying it was backstage she didn't like?"

"Right. She wanted to be a singer. You know, the night club kind. A little jazzy, a little bluesy."

While she spoke she half smiled. Her eyes were on his, judging, testing, the way she always did.

"You know where she lives when she's not traveling the circuit?"

"She's from the south somewhere. Memphis, maybe. Maybe not." Margot looked away. "I miss you."

"I think about you a lot," Cross said.

"But you won't go so far as to say you miss me too?" she said, playing, flirting.

But he knew her, knew it wasn't as light-hearted as it seemed.

"I don't want to say that because I don't know where that would lead me."

"I'm off it," she said.

"What?"

"All of it. I mean I drink, but the other stuff? It's out of my life." She was trying to read his face. He could tell she wanted to find out if that mattered.

"Good."

"Look, I'm in town until the race. I don't work every night."

He didn't know what to say. He didn't know what to do. The urge to run away battled with the urge to kiss her. The bad thing was that he knew she knew exactly what was going on in his mind. Nobody knew him better than she did, or at least no one could draw him into a game like she did.

"You seeing anybody?" she asked amidst the silence.

"No. No, I'm not."

"Live in the same place?"

For a fleeting moment, he thought about lying. "Yes."

"I love that place."

"Yeah."

"Why don't you hang around," she said, tossing her hair, preparing to move on, relenting. "Maybe some of the other girls know a little more about Norah."

She walked away.

He felt the same way he felt when they broke up. Empty.

Nine

With the rest of the afternoon free, Shanahan decided now was as good a time as any to introduce attorney and client. The "little murderer," as Kowalski called him, had taken leave from work when his name was first introduced to the media. He was home, bored, anxious, angry, willing, and wanting to get on with it, but wondering what "it" was.

What Shanahan hadn't counted on was putting his 70-year-old body on the back of a Harley Road King. As Kowalski had explained it, he bought his first Harley after seeing Fonda and Hopper in *Easy Rider*. He had owned several over the years. This one was for the old road warriors, giving in a bit to comfort, but holding up the tradition, still giving the world the low, testosterone growl of a real Harley engine.

"C'mon, live a little," he said, seeing Shanahan weighing potential consequences.

"That's what I'm thinking about."

Shanahan's legs were a little unsteady when he dismounted in front of the Silk Factory. But he liked the sensation. One rarely gets a chance to move that fast so much *in* the world he is passing through. It was a different sensation than riding in his ancient Chevy Malibu.

"You ought to get yourself one," Kowalski said in front of Evans's building. Shanahan pressed the button to announce their arrival.

"You remember we talked about this," Shanahan said, trying to phrase what he was about to say the most careful way possible. "If this comes to trial, you might not be the one to represent him."

"I know," he said. "You'll get one of those bastards who tap dance on marble floors. Hey, let's just wait and see how the chips fall. You may want me. You may not."

By the time the three of them were done talking, Shanahan was exhausted. Kowalski was exhausting just by his presence. You never forgot he was in the room, even when someone else had the floor.

Shanahan was glad to be home. He fixed a whiskey and water, and began to cook dinner. Casey was outside watching Maureen water the lawn, occasionally dodging a mischievous misdirection of the spray. Einstein was asleep on the chair where the late day's sun still sent a shaft of light.

Shanahan took a sip of his drink. All was well with the world, at least this evening.

Cross looked at the clock radio. 4:06 glowed in the dark. That's when the knock came. He knew who it was. He knew what was going to happen. He had slept lightly, fitfully knowing, hoping and hating that this would happen.

He knew Margot hated those hours after work, when night headed into twilight. As she once told him, if she could just have a man between four and seven in the morning, she'd be a happy girl.

Cross didn't bother to turn the light on or to grab a robe. He opened the door for her, turned and headed back to bed. She knew her way. In a moment, he heard her clothes rustle, and could make out the slender silhouette of her shape in the dimmest of light.

He hadn't felt this kind of anticipation since he was a teen and Lisa Turner slipped off her bikini in the back seat of his Ford. The moment Margot's body touched his, it was as if her absence in the last two years was erased; and he had seen her yesterday or the day before. The touch was familiar. The scent was familiar.

The only sounds came from flesh touching flesh, perhaps a slight moan of pleasure. For a few moments, the anger he felt at Channing, the panic he had with his finances, and the pain he carried from an earlier Margot went away. Her hands brought him to life, his kisses calmed her.

Inside her, he felt wonderfully lost. He could barely endure that exquisite moment when pain and pleasure were indistinguishable.

Cross didn't remember falling asleep; and when he awoke, he wondered if he had dreamt it all. Margot wasn't there. He called out to her, slowly got out of bed and went through the rooms.

Ah, there was a cigarette, crushed out on a small plate on the counter in the kitchen. Other than that, there wasn't a trace.

Cross retreated to the bedroom, pulled the blinds closed so that very little light came into the room. He climbed back into bed. Another trace. Her scent lingered. The moment was as painful as it was delicious. He slept.

Shanahan slipped out of bed as quietly as he could. Maureen slumbered, her body facing away from him. Into the kitchen for the morning ritual. Let Casey out. Feed Einstein. Make coffee. Unfold the morning newspaper. Todd Evans's face stared back. Beside his portrait was one of Lianna Bailey. In the caption, she was listed as victim and he as suspect.

It was official. Shanahan was glad the young man had benefit of counsel the afternoon before. Guilty or not, Todd was entitled to a little guidance as he walked the path dodging landmines set by the police and grenades from the press.

Shanahan sat down as the coffee maker gurgled and hissed its way to a finish. He focused on the second paragraph of the story on Lianna's disappearance:

A spokesperson for the Indianapolis Police Department (IPD) today said that Todd Evans, 28, is the leading suspect in the disappearance of Lianna Bailey, 30, an executive at Noah Rose & Company. Evans, who lived with Bailey in a condominium in the Lockerbie neighborhood for nearly three years, is a vice president at Masters, Credlin and Hawkins, an Indianapolis-based financial investment firm.

Shanahan didn't know Evans was a VP. He was doing pretty well for his age all on his own, perhaps not as much in Lianna's shadow as her aunt suggested. He also noticed they called Bailey an executive, not an executive assistant which would have required the story to include the name of the executive she assisted—Mr. Bradley Gray Pedersen. He scanned the article. The IPD spokesperson was Max Rafferty, who said the police would pursue the investigation as a missing persons case, but that they did not discount foul play.

The reasons they gave for looking so seriously at Todd Evans were the insurance policy, indications that they weren't getting along, and the fact that he was the last person known to have seen her alive. Pretty standard stuff—except that Lianna purportedly boarded a plane for San Francisco.

Shanahan moved from the paper to the coffee maker. He poured himself a cup. He looked out through the back door but failed to see that Casey was begging to be let back in. Shanahan was staring at Pedersen's face. How could he make sure the police wouldn't put blinders on now that they had someone in their sights, and fail to make all the possible connections that would lead elsewhere, particularly to Pedersen?

Cross went back to the computer. He was going to spend more time on Noah Rose & Company's website and on the Mason Life Systems website. He wanted to know more and he was happy to focus on something other than Margot and Channing. They were, in different ways, his current demons. Sitting around the house in his state of mind wasn't going to do him any good. There were some other things he could do. The best thing that came out of his brief liaison with Margot was that he did get more information from the other dancers because she was there and made it seem all right.

Norah was Elizabeth Jefferson of Biloxi, Mississippi. She had family there. She worked hard on her singing career, but it wasn't going anywhere. She had three agents and none seemed to be able to land her a record deal or a gig in a respectable place. None of the girls seemed to think her sudden departure indicated anything bad. In fact they didn't think it was all that sudden to Norah. It was as if a deal came through. No doubt in their minds, she got a better offer. "She was happy as could be," one dancer told Cross, "during her last night here. She was singing and laughing and told a couple of girls she was going."

She stayed at a hotel on the corner of 16th and Meridian. Cross knew the place. He'd inquire. He'd also call information in Biloxi and see if he could find family.

At four in the afternoon, Shanahan went to Harry's place. Harry was speaking Spanish to a laughing audience of Hispanics. Shanahan sat at the bar and wondered if they were laughing at Harry's stories or his miserable Spanish. The group was probably Mexican. In the last few years, the neighborhood was changing. New groups were moving in. And Harry loved the idea there was a whole new population who hadn't heard his stories.

Kowalski arrived on time.

"Damn," Harry said, leaving the stage for a moment. "You look like an emissary from the Mafia. I don't know which one, Irish, Italian, or Russian, but you are one scary guy."

Kowalski grabbed Harry and hugged him.

"You've gotten old and fat," Harry said.

"And you shrank, lost what little ass you had. You've become a leprechaun."

The three of them settled into a booth in the back.

Shanahan ordered a Miller. Kowalski seemed to be pondering the decision.

"How about a nice little Pinot Noir?" he asked Harry.

"Peeeno what?"

"It's a nice, light red wine."

"Wine, he says." Harry shook his head. "I got red wine and I got white wine. It's pretty well aged. The bottles have been here for thirty years 'cause nobody that comes into this bar wants a stinkin' glass of wine."

"Give me a Scotch. You pick it, Harry. I dare not ask," Kowalski said, grinning.

"Scotch has probably been around awhile too," Shanahan said.

"This place hasn't changed a bit," Kowalski said. "I half expect to see Delaney behind the bar."

"He's probably sittin' at a bar right now," Harry said, "only there's palm trees and half-naked women around."

"What about the stew? You still serving stew?"

"Delaney's own. I'll get you a bowl, tide a man like you over until dinner."

Harry left. Kowalski noticed the look on Shanahan's face.

"Oh, really?"

"It probably won't kill you," Shanahan said.

Maureen arrived to a happy greeting from Harry, who was busy fixing drinks.

"And for you?"

"Rum and tonic, twist of lemon," she said. "Light on the rum."

"Whatever you say."

She squeezed in beside Shanahan, kissed him on the cheek.

"I didn't know you had a daughter," Kowalski said sincerely.

"I don't."

"My God, yours?" Kowalski asked, surprised.

"Bought and paid for, right out of the catalog," Shanahan said.

"I'm sorry, that was all a little insensitive," Kowalski said, looking at Maureen as he spoke. Then he just shook his head.

Harry arrived with the bowl of stew.

"And so you're being punished for your sins," Shanahan said.

"You going to San Francisco?" Kowalski asked Shanahan.

Maureen's eyes widened.

"No point. I can't just walk the streets hoping to spot a woman I saw in a photograph," Shanahan said. "I need a place to start. A charge on her Visa, something from her cell phone. For all we know, she could have landed in San Francisco, and hopped a cruise to Timbuktu. Can you get something from the cops or the DA?"

Harry brought the drinks. "Pinot Noir," Harry said, curling his lip.

Kowalski considered the request. "Maybe. They'll dodge and stonewall, especially this early in the investigation."

"What I really want is to get to Pedersen." Shanahan stared at Kowalski. "Can't you do a discovery?"

"I could find a way."

Kowalski took a bite of his stew and smiled bravely.

"You don't like Pedersen?" he asked.

"No," Shanahan said.

"Whatever we do, we have to counter Rafferty's PR attack on Evans," Kowalski said. "I'll get on that right away."

"You want the press?"

"Of course. I love the press when they write about me. That's why I agreed to do this. For what I'm getting paid, I couldn't keep myself in cigars."

"So, what do you plan to do?" Cross asked.

"A press conference. I mean the victim bought a ticket. With airport security like it is, that should put a hitch in Rafferty's giddyup." Kowalski grinned.

73

Ten

Shanahan spent the night with his regrets. He'd called in Kowalski for one reason, so he could stay on the case. Now, Kowalski was not only running the show but seemed to think it ought to be a P. T. Barnum kind of show. In the morning, Shanahan felt better about it. By making himself so public, Kowalski would have some leverage to get police records and, more important to Shanahan, put pressure on Pedersen to meet and answer some questions. Something Shanahan could no longer do. Put those questions in the public eye and Pedersen would have to answer them. Reporters would note if he refused to answer.

By morning Shanahan came to not only like the idea of a press conference, he also wanted to be part of it. Not usually one for the spotlight, Shanahan wanted Rafferty to notice. He also wanted Pedersen to notice. Perhaps, he thought, he also wanted Jennifer Bailey to notice. Shanahan didn't like to be shoved around, and he'd like these folks to know he wasn't shoved very far at all.

May in Indianapolis. It's not exactly New Orleans during Mardi Gras. No one gets a strand of beads as reward for a flash of breast—or any other body part for that matter. Overt drunkenness is contained in parking lots and makeshift RV settlements near the Speedway. The obligatory downtown parade is nice enough, but isn't so edgy that it would offend the Family Research Council. Overall, the debauchery is seedy, rather than decadent, in the midwestern tradition. But Indianapolis during the last days of May is still a city hooked on speed and excitement.

74

Shanahan sensed this kind of electric atmosphere as James Fenimore Kowalski placed a lectern just below the western steps of Monument Circle in preparation for his 11:00 A.M. press conference. "Indianapolis 500" banners hung from the lampposts and the Circle was filled with tourists. At 10:45 the press converged, eager to tape for the noon news. Crossing the brick paved street, on their way to set up, were camera operators lugging gear. Vans from the four local television stations occupied space on the other side, ready to beam the signal. Kowalski had pulled it off. Passersby, who probably had no notion of what was happening, paused to see what the commotion was about.

This time of year, one might expect to see a few celebrities in the city. Paul Newman, James Garner, David Letterman, people with ties to the city or ties to racing. Was all the fuss about some movie star?

"Looks like quite a turnout," Shanahan said to Kowalski, who was settling in behind the podium.

"Let's just hope that there are no auto accidents or fires for the rest of the day."

Shanahan had no doubt that, short of a major catastrophe, this was the story of the day—at least locally. Any further developments and it could go national.

Evans arrived. Half a dozen camera lenses aimed at him.

"Stand to the left and slightly behind me during the conference," Kowalski told him. "Answer no questions and whatever you do, don't show any expression whatsoever no matter what I say or what others say. Don't laugh. Don't cry. Don't look anything."

Evans nodded.

"You have your prepared statement?" Kowalski asked the younger man.

"Yes."

"OK, I'll make a few remarks, introduce you. You read the statement. Read it word for word. When you're finished, step back. I'll do the rest of the talking."

Evans nodded again. He understood. He wore a gray suit,

white shirt, and a pale blue tie. He was a handsome young man. Shanahan tried to picture him doing someone else harm. He didn't see it. Then again, there have been some innocent-looking and mighty charming killers.

Microphones were attached to the podium. At 11:00 A.M. Kowalski started to speak, but noticed a straggler—a cameraman without call letters approaching. He'd wait until the guy was set up. Could be a stringer for CNN. You never knew. Kowalski glanced at Shanahan. Shanahan moved up just behind Evans, put his hand on Evans's shoulder. Evans looked at him, gave a faint smile and took a deep breath the way someone who'd just stopped crying would. Shanahan eyed Lt. Rafferty as Kowalski began to speak.

"We're here today because the Indianapolis Police Department has started a campaign to convict Todd Evans of foul play in the disappearance of Lianna Bailey," Kowalski said. "This trial by TV poisons a public that might be called upon to serve on a jury. This trial by TV destroys the life of a young, innocent man. No evidence. No arraignment. This is an abuse of justice by those people entrusted to preserve it. As Mr. Evans's attorney, I would be remiss if I did not defend Mr. Evans from this disgusting attempt to convict before anyone has even begun to hear the evidence."

Rafferty shook his head. Shanahan looked around for Lt. Swann. A no show.

"Mr. Evans is going to read a brief statement," Kowalski continued, "then I will have a few comments, and then I will take your questions. Mr. Evans?"

Todd Evans moved hesitantly to the podium. He didn't look at the crowd that seemed to be expanding by the second. He looked down at his notes.

"I am deeply upset by the disappearance of Lianna Bailey," Todd said flatly. "We have been together for nearly three years. Like any couple we have had disagreements, but we have always worked them out. Lianna, if you are out there somewhere, please call. I miss you. I promise that I will cooperate with any and all investigations into Lianna's disappearance. Thank you."

Todd stepped back with more enthusiasm than he used stepping forward. Shanahan hoped that the flatness of his speech was due to nervousness rather than just not having the ability to lie with conviction.

Questions came from the reporters immediately, but Kowalski put his hands up as if to halt a train.

"Todd is not answering any questions. I will, if you have any."

"What about the insurance policy—?"

Kowalski didn't let the reporter finish.

"Todd Evans took out a policy on Lianna Bailey. That much the police leaked to the media. What Lieutenant Rafferty didn't tell you is that Lianna took out a policy in the same amount on Todd. The two of them had plans to purchase a house together, an expensive house. In order to protect the other's ability to live at that high level without a two-person income such a policy was wise."

"Why would a person with so much going for her, leave?" asked the same reporter, a blond anchor for one of the network affiliates.

"We don't know the answer to that," Kowalski said. "We do know that a ticket was purchased on American Trans Air for San Francisco and that her car was found at the airport."

"But do we know it was her?"

"With airport security being what it is these days, why don't you try to fly to San Francisco with someone else's name?"

The questions and answers went on for half an hour. Shanahan wandered into the crowd and next to Rafferty.

"Hi," Shanahan said.

"What have you got against me?" Rafferty said.

"How much time do you have?"

"One day the luck of the Irish is going to do a Dixie on you," Rafferty said.

"Not looking for luck, just a little honesty."

The two of them stopped talking when it appeared Kowalski was about to make his final statement.

"That's all of the questions for today," Kowalski said. "One more thing though. We're not going to allow the city or anyone else to railroad this decent young man. I have an investigator working on the case. He will be interviewing everyone, friends, neighbors, and all of the people she worked with. We are asking the police or the District Attorney's office to share with us any information that could effect the eventual outcome of the investigation—" here Kowalski smiled—"including all the people who worked with her at Noah Rose Company." He nodded a thank you at the press and the crowd and stepped back to talk with Evans.

"It's not in court yet," Rafferty said quietly to Shanahan.

"But you made it public. You've already ruined this kid's life."

"He did it. You can take it to the bank."

"So where is Lieutenant Swann in all of this?"

"This isn't his case."

"Whose is it?"

"Mine. All mine," he said, mimicking an old-time villain. "You screw with me and this time you're taking on a lot more than the police department. Words to the wise and I am confident you'll pay them no heed." Rafferty punched Shanahan gently on the shoulder. "You know I think I might enjoy that even more, know what I mean?"

Shanahan punched Rafferty just above the heart, much harder.

"You hit me once," said Rafferty. "I haven't forgotten. I promise you'll be sorry if you ever do it again."

Rafferty glared; but there were too many cameras around.

Shanahan smiled. He knew Rafferty wouldn't risk doing anything in public. Some other time, alone, in the dark of night, things could be different.

Kowalski, who had kept Todd from talking to the media, had already parked the frightened young man on the back of his Harley and they roared off. The crowd was dispersing. Maureen had three appointments to show houses in the afternoon. Shanahan wasn't sure if it was adrenaline or a random dose of testosterone; but he wasn't ready to go home. He'd stop by Harry's.

Mid-afternoon, aside from the regulars who tended to sit quietly, eyes either on their beer or on whatever was on television, there was Todd Evans. He looked up, but Shanahan knew better than to speak while Harry was in the middle of one of his stories.

Harry looked up. "I was just telling my friend here about my nasty Uncle Walter."

Shanahan knew the story. Harry was always glad when someone new came in because he hadn't updated his story file in awhile. Probably hadn't for the last decade.

"You'da had to have known Walter. He'd pinch a penny until it turned into a dime kind of guy. I mean the man was obsessed with money. He did nothing with it, except save it. He had money buried in the yard, stuck in the walls, in mattresses. It was a terrible insanity this man had. Then, as is always the case, Walter's wife was a saint. She waited on him hand and foot. She made soap by hand to save him money. Used the tea bags over until there wasn't a hint of color let alone flavor left."

Harry looked up to see that everyone was paying attention.

"Well, the day came," Harry said, "as it does for all of us. Thing is he had fair warning. Walter, on his deathbed, he called his wife to his side. And Uncle Walter made her promise on the grave of her mother, that she'd bury all the money with him. 'Put it in a box, woman, and put the box in the coffin.' Well, she was beside herself. The only money they had, he was claiming as his and his alone. 'What will I live on?' she asked. 'You'll be on your own now. But I made the money myself and I'm taking it with me. You promise you'll put my fortune in a box and put that box in that coffin and see to it that it goes into the ground with me?' She couldn't bring herself to deny him his dying wish. 'I will,' she said. 'On your mother's grave?' he demanded. 'On my mother's grave,' she replied."

A call came out over the bar for a Budweiser. Harry was

upset, but he fetched the beer for the guy on the stool by the door. Shanahan thought that poor Todd looked trapped.

"You knew I'd be here?" Shanahan asked, clearly puzzled.

"No, I didn't know where to go," Evans said. "I didn't want to run into anyone I knew . . . I mean . . . who knew me and Lianna."

Shanahan nodded as Harry returned to pick up the thread of his story.

"There they were on the day of Walter's burial. And the wife, Mildred was her name, picked up a wooden box and slipped it inside the casket. 'You're not really going to put all his money in the casket?' Mildred's sister asked. 'Sure. That's what he wanted. Thing is,' Mildred said, 'I couldn't fit all his money in a box that would also fit in the coffin, so I hope he don't mind, I put the money in the bank, and wrote him a check.'"

It took Todd Evans a moment, but he laughed. That was good enough for Harry.

Harry was off and, without being asked, opened a bottle of beer for Shanahan.

"Since we're both here," Shanahan said to Evans, who was nursing a Coke, "we might as well talk. Who do you think is telling the police that you didn't want the baby?"

"Don't know."

"Why is Jennifer Bailey withdrawing her support?"

"I don't know that either. Maybe they can't imagine anyone else doing it. I don't know."

Sometimes Shanahan didn't like himself very well. Evans came here to get away from the problems not to be faced with them. But some things need to be explained.

"Do you suppose this is something Lianna told her sister?"

"I suppose it's possible," Evans answered. "But they didn't talk much to each other."

Shanahan thought he might want to talk with Jasmine.

"Why not?" Shanahan asked.

"There were some jealousies. Their aunt . . ."

"Jennifer Bailey."

"Yes. She had grown weary supporting Jasmine. She was always in trouble. Taking in strays. People. Troubled people. And then those people would get her in trouble. Mrs. Bailey kept saying Jasmine should be more like Lianna, who she thought was more like her. Ambitious. Going for the prize. That kind of thing. Jasmine thought Lianna was superficial and selfish."

"Did you get along with Jasmine?"

"Didn't see her much," Evans said. "We got along."

"Did you get along with their aunt?"

"We were always polite, but I'm pretty sure she thought her niece could do a whole lot better than me."

"You're doing well," Shanahan said.

"Mrs. Bailey thought Lianna should be with someone who has already made it. A governor, someone who inherited wealth, or a CEO of a huge corporation."

"Someone like Pedersen?"

"Yes, I suppose."

"What was her relationship with Pedersen? Could it have been more than boss and employee?"

"It was more than that. But if you mean was it sex or romance . . ."

"Yeah, that's what I mean," Shanahan said, pushing through Evans's reluctance to let that thought continue.

"Everything is possible, isn't it?"

There was quiet for a moment, except for the rattling of glasses as Harry washed them a few feet away.

"People who I thought were my friends," Evans said, "are uncomfortable with me now. They don't say anything. They're nice to me. But there is a wall now. Formal, distant. They can't get away quick enough. Even on the phone."

Shanahan didn't know what to say. He didn't know how to make him feel better. Shanahan knew the young man's life was changed forever. It didn't make any difference if he was cleared, if the abductor was found, or even if she returned alive and well. Evans's life had taken a turn. He would never be able to go back.

Eleven

C ross watched the press conference from home. By three in the afternoon, he'd consumed a bag of potato chips and several cups of coffee. He'd switched channels so often it looked like he was playing a computer game. There was a program devoted to the benefits of consuming mammoth doses of calcium, sponsored by a company that made a calcium product. The show looked like a talk show, where the interviewer appeared to be a disinterested party.

Uplifting, he thought. Free TV. They were giving up on the whole idea of programming: just run commercials. He rubbed his palm over his unshaved cheek. He was feeling sorry for himself. Because that idiot Channing screwed him out of his fee. Because last night was a one-night stand with someone he had feelings for. Because he didn't know if he could make the mortgage, let alone the car payment. Details.

All along Shanahan wanted the young man to be innocent because he liked him, because he seemed like a decent guy, and because he never really liked helping criminals get away with their crimes. What could make it worse than just being wrong about Todd Evans would be Shanahan swallowing a sad story on top of it.

He arrived home before Maureen, played ball with Casey, and began dinner. Pieces of chicken sausage and blanched vegetables would find themselves in a big iron skillet with rice. He'd make a coleslaw. Maureen would be in a good mood. She liked it when Shanahan cooked.

The evening promised to be good. The Cubs were playing

in San Francisco. They would be up late. The game didn't start until nine. But Shanahan liked the Giants' ballpark and he liked watching the two teams play.

Shanahan had all the ingredients prepared, but Maureen was running late. He'd wait to fire up the burners. He decided to use the time to call Lianna's sister, Jasmine. He tried the number he had from a case that was closed more than a year ago. Disconnected. He tried information. There was a number for a J. Bailey. That could be Jennifer; but he doubted if the Attorney General's home phone was listed. He would try it.

"Jasmine?" Shanahan asked when he heard the "hello."

"Yes," came a cautious reply.

"This is Shanahan."

"My aunt said not to talk to you."

"She's already talked to you about me?"

"Yes."

"And you always do what your aunt asks."

"What do you want?" Her voice was cool.

"I want to know what you think about Lianna's disappearance."

"Look, you were nice to Luke, I appreciate it. But . . ."

"How is Luke?" Shanahan asked, not only wanting to know, but also wanting to keep her on the phone.

"Struggling," she said. "I think he's kicked the drugs, but he's struggling with life. I guess we all are, one way or another. We're still together, if that's what you're asking."

Shanahan thought about asking her to pass along his good wishes, but decided against it. He wasn't good at small, polite, hopeful chatter.

"Are you going to talk to me about Lianna?" he asked.

"I saw you at the press conference. On television."

"I was there," Shanahan said. "Are you one of those who believe Todd had something to do with this?"

"I don't know what to think."

"Did Lianna talk to you about their relationship, about any other relationship, anything she might have feared?"

"She tells me nothing."

"You are sisters. You grew up together. You might not love each other, but you know each other. Would she just take off like that, without telling anyone?"

"If someone offered her fame and fortune, she wouldn't worry about a little old thing like 'goodbye.'"

"It's possible, then?"

"Yeah," Jasmine said, and after a pause continued. "Mr. Shanahan, she could make you really want to kill her. That's all I have for today."

It seemed to Shanahan that all the Bailey girls were tough as nails. Someone else might be a little more concerned about a missing and quite possibly dead sister. Someone else might be a little more circumspect about incriminating herself. This was Jasmine. She pulled no punches.

Maureen came home exhausted, thrilled that Shanahan was taking care of dinner, that there was a long lazy evening ahead of her. One of the reasons she liked baseball so much was that she could do other things, browse through the home magazines, or read a light mystery and still keep track of what was going on.

Sunk deep in an old upholstered chair, Maureen thumbed through a magazine. The Cubs were changing pitchers and that always took awhile.

"I think you need to talk to the Schmidt girl," Maureen said.

"Lianna's friend? She didn't know much."

"She didn't say much. It's hard for me to believe that Lianna, no matter how self-sufficient she was, didn't confide in someone. You say the sisters weren't close, so it almost has to be her best friend. If it's not Mary Beth, perhaps Lianna has another 'best' friend."

"You saw it. I didn't connect," Shanahan said. "She was polite, but she looked at me as if I was a security guard at the airport. Something to endure."

"Maybe Howie's charms might prove helpful."

"Are you saying I'm short in the charm department?"

"Look who you have by your side," Maureen said, grinning.

"I must have more subtle charms, I guess, for the connoisseur."

"Yes, like a fine wine," she said, lifting her nose in the air. "Only those with exquisite taste can appreciate . . ." She let the sentence trail off with a sensuous shrug of her shoulders. Shanahan was thinking vinegar. He knew he came across a little sour sometimes.

"Evans can't afford a lawyer and two private detectives. I've already asked Howie to do a few things for me for free. I can't ask him to do more. I'll do it." He would call tomorrow. He returned his thoughts to the game, though they would return again and again to Todd. Shanahan didn't know what to think about the young man.

It wasn't *déjà vu*, but it could have been. At 4:07, his eyes opened. There was a knock at the door. This time he slipped on his robe. He wouldn't do this. They would talk briefly. She would go. He switched on the lamp, then flicked the switch for the porch light.

It cast a dim luminescence on Margot's face. She knew Howie's intent.

"Can't we just spend a few hours from time to time?" She wore a gray sweatshirt and jeans. No make-up.

"Margot—"

"Without having to commit to a lifetime." She nudged past him and into the room. "Nothing in this world is really constant and forever." She pulled the sweatshirt over her head. "Why pretend?"

"Listen—"

"Are you really going to throw me out?"

"You know I can't do that," he said, resigned. He could fight off the sexual impulses, but he couldn't muster the coldness to send her away. "Sleep," he said. "Just sleep."

It wasn't quite light when the phone rang, interrupting Shanahan's dance with a naked headless woman on a beach at night.

85

"Yes," Shanahan said, adjusting to his new, more comforting place in the world.

"It's Swann."

"OK."

"They're going to arrest him."

"When?"

"Maybe now. Maybe later, but not much later. I don't know, but they're taking him in."

"What did they find?"

"The baby isn't his."

"What?"

"Not his. Isn't his kid," Swann said, irritated.

"How do they know?"

"Medical records. He had that little operation where they go snip snip."

"Jesus," Shanahan said, looking over at Maureen. She hadn't moved an inch. "Whose kid is it?"

"Don't know. Just know whose it isn't."

"You back on the case?" Shanahan asked.

"No. And you didn't talk to me."

"Swann?"

"I have to go. I'll be in touch."

Swann was the straightest shooting, by-the-book cop Shanahan had ever met. As welcomed as it was, this was very strange behavior.

Shanahan slipped quietly from bed and went into the kitchen. Einstein followed him in, but saw that his benefactor went to the phone instead of the refrigerator. He walked out with apparent disdain. Shanahan tried to call Kowalski, but he only had the lawyer's office number. He'd have to correct that.

The next morning, Cross found Margot, fully dressed, sitting at his desk. At least three cigarettes had been crushed on a small lunch plate.

"I made coffee," she said, without looking up.

Cross went to the kitchen, poured himself a cup and returned. She looked up. "Thanks," she said. "It's important that I know I can count on someone somewhere. I won't ask for much. Just a few hours now and then."

Maybe he was adult enough to handle a few hours here and there and not want more.

"Now and then." He touched her shoulder.

"I travel a lot."

"How long are you going to keep traveling?"

She smiled. "Until I'm all traveled out."

Shanahan was unable to sleep after the call from Swann. After an hour or so of trying to drift off, he got up again, he let Casey out, fed Einstein, fixed coffee. The day was heating up already. He hoped it wouldn't be humid.

The morning paper was at the front door. Nothing on Lianna. It was all about the race.

He switched on TV to get the morning news. Weather—it wouldn't be humid—traffic reports, weather, traffic reports, the race, weather, traffic reports. Nothing on Lianna.

It was still early. He'd wait until 9 A.M., then he'd call Kowalski. He wanted to call Todd Evans, but decided not to. He didn't want everyone to know that Swann had warned him, that he had someone on the inside.

Kowalski answered. When he heard Shanahan's voice, he didn't bother with the pleasantries.

"They have him. I got the one call. He's been arrested and by now he's wearing a little orange suit."

"What are you going to do?"

"Talk to him. See about bail. Then see the DA, see what the charges are, though I'm pretty sure I know."

"If he's up for murder, can he get bail?" Shanahan asked.

"In this case maybe. They were lovers, which means there's not a high probability he would kill anyone else. It's not like he's some sort of serial sniper. And one big problem they have is they don't have Lianna's body."

"Something else you should know," Shanahan said. "It wasn't his kid."

87

"Shit," Kowalski said. Then he laughed. "That works both ways. Sure a guy finds out his girlfriend is pregnant with another guy and it pisses him off big time. But there's another mystery. Who went off to San Francisco? This plays out that she ran off to be with the guy who fathered her child. Could mean that someone else had a motive. Lots of possibilities."

"But Evans lied," Shanahan said.

"What? He said he loved you. You had sex. And now he never calls?"

"You know what I mean," Shanahan said. He had sounded a bit naïve. "Don't tell Evans what we know yet. Let's see if he tells us."

Twelve

Shanahan called Miss Schmidt at work and was surprised she had to get through two people screening her calls. Mary Beth told him she had already said all that she was going to say.

"I'm sorry. I really don't want to sound threatening," Shanahan said, "but I can get a court order and this can be done in a less than friendly environment. As I said, I'm working for Mr. Evans's attorney, Miss Schmidt, and we're just trying to learn a bit more about Lianna."

"I told you everything the other day," she said, "what little I know."

"It will only take a few moments," Shanahan said. "There's a new development."

"Oh my God! Is she all right?"

"Don't know. Could be. She's still missing. Unless you know something I don't know."

"I know what the police say."

"If Mr. Evans is a murderer, so be it. But wouldn't it be horrible if he didn't do it and the real killer is roaming around somewhere posing a danger to someone else? You maybe. I know you know things you didn't tell me before."

"I think the police have the killer." She said it abruptly as if the words just leapt off a cliff.

"Well see, we didn't talk about that before, you and I. Let's meet and get it over with, or we can make this a really big deal. Newspapers, TV."

"If I talk with you, will you keep the media out of this?"

"I won't talk to them about this, I promise," he said, hedging. "On the other hand, I can't promise anything if I can't have a few minutes with you."

He said this though he had no idea what else he could ask her that hadn't just been discussed. Hope without basis. On the off chance she would slip up or he would be struck with a moment of brilliance. Had never happened before. He was due, he thought.

"I'll meet you some place public, with people around."

"I don't blame you. At your convenience."

"Same place."

"Yes."

"After work?"

"Right," she said, defeated. "Better make it at least six. It's not a good day for me to get away. I've got my work and Lianna's work to do."

"I didn't know you worked together that closely."

"I'm the only one who knows her job," she said.

Maybe he did get something after all.

For Shanahan, the days seemed short and unproductive. Evans was in jail. The trail was cold. Unless Shanahan could come up with some alternative avenue to investigate, the steamroller was headed in Todd Evans's direction at a steady pace. Shanahan felt powerless to stop it. The police had all the resources. What Evans had was a down-on-his-luck ex-cop, a semi-retired private investigator and a renegade lawyer who thought he was a Hell's Angel. What they all had in common was that they were poor, blunt and not too fond of authority and up against a state attorney general, a powerful CEO, then maybe the district attorney and the police force.

When he got back to the kitchen, Einstein had absconded with a small stalk of broccoli. He would eat anything. So would Casey. Except for grapes. Casey didn't seem to know what to do with a grape, holding it delicately in his teeth, looking confused and a little frightened.

He wrote a note to Maureen to say he was meeting with Schmidt. He didn't invite her along this time.

Tippi Hedren, Kim Novak, Grace Kelly, maybe Martha Hyer. Mary Beth Schmidt, in the mind of Deets Shanahan, was one of those cold, impenetrable blondes Alfred Hitchcock featured in his films.

"Mary Beth?" Shanahan asked as he approached.

"Sit down," she said, somewhere between a welcome and an order.

"Thanks for meeting with me," he said without warmth.

She nodded impatiently.

"I came out of courtesy but I can't imagine how I can help you. I've told the police everything I know. I told you everything I know."

"You told the police that Todd Evans didn't want the baby, right?"

"Did the police tell you that?" She seemed shocked, but he was intrigued by her response.

"Does the truth change based on who told me?" he asked. Shanahan knew the best way to get the answers was to put the interviewee on the defensive. He only suspected that she was the one who talked to the police about Todd and Lianna's problems. Now he was pretty sure she was the one. She could have protested, but she didn't. She stayed quiet.

"When did she tell you about Todd and the baby?"

"I don't remember when."

Confirmed.

"Do you remember when she told you she was having an affair?" It was a safe gamble. If she knew about the baby, she had to know more about the relationship that created the child.

She raised her head, jutted out her chin in defiance. The effect was that she was now looking down on him. He didn't know whether he'd struck the truth or revealed his tactics. She looked both pouty and superior.

"It wasn't Todd's child, you know that?" he asked, softening only a little.

91

She looked around as if there might be someone to come to her rescue.

"I don't have a lot of time, here. Can you fill me in or not?"

"About what?"

"About everything. Was she happy at work? Was someone threatening her? Was she seeing someone? Did she have a relationship with Pedersen?"

"I came down here on good faith," she said, standing, eyes flashing.

"I'm asking in good faith."

"You're not being honest with me," she said. "You're trying to trap me into something."

"You've not leveled at all. I need to know some things. One of them is about Lianna and Pedersen. Are you going to help or not?"

She gave him a cold, hard stare. She was tough. She wasn't holding back tears. She was holding back rage.

"I'm going to find out who went to San Francisco."

She looked at him defiantly, a cold smile crossing her lips.

"I'm going to find out whose baby she was carrying," Shanahan said, not allowing his glee to show as her smile disappeared instantly.

She moved through the tables quickly and the eyes that followed her out came back to him.

Cross nibbled at some Monterey Jack cheese. The television flickered in the darkness and his eyes were directed to the screen, but the images didn't register. He was having conversations with Margot, though she wasn't there. Not a healthy sign, he thought when he realized what he was doing. He should go to bed, but he knew better. He would wait up for her. He wouldn't drink anything. That would fog up his mind and encourage sleep to seduce him.

He waited. He walked outside in the still night. He paced in the kitchen, sipping coffee. He thumbed through magazines he'd read before. He waited, and waited some more.

At 3 A.M. he heard her approach the house. She didn't.

Though the last two nights she arrived shortly after four, he became angry at her tardiness at a little past three. He bawled her out. He wished he'd gotten her cell phone number just to be sure. The big hand on the clock in the kitchen slipped past four, four fifteen, four thirty. He was wired. She wasn't coming. But he was sure he wouldn't sleep now even if he crawled into bed. Or he'd sleep forever.

Cross put on a CD of the Rolling Stones. He was feeling sad and sorry for himself. He knew that. He thought he ought to enjoy it.

The album was a mix of blues and psychedelic, he'd first heard when he was a kid and raided his older brother's record collection. "Lady Jane." "Let it Bleed." Finally, "It's All Over Now."

A little after five, he understood. They didn't have a date. These were his expectations. Only his. She made no promises. Just because she came over twice didn't mean she'd ever come over again or if she did, it might be six months from now or tomorrow night. Cross had never done heroin, but he understood how, after getting over her finally a few years ago, he was still addicted. Just a little taste of her brought it all back. Full force. Was she that powerful? Was he that weak?

Maybe he should feel flattered, Cross thought. Margot gave herself to him freely. The others paid for her time and attention. He didn't feel flattered. Instead he felt jealousy of whatever she shared for any reason with anyone else. And he knew if Cross was her haven in Indianapolis, somebody easily might be playing that role in Cleveland or St. Louis.

She wasn't good for him. Why couldn't he tell her "no?" Why couldn't he stop wanting her?

He watched the sky lighten. It looked like he'd face another day without a night's sleep to restore his energy. What would he do now? There didn't seem to be much point to anything. To sleep or not to sleep, that was the question.

Cross decided to skip sleep. While it would be a great way to throw away a few unpleasant hours of consciousness, it would throw off the rhythm and he'd be up all the next night as well. He clicked on the TV, in time for the early-morning news not because he was interested but because it would be a narcotic.

After the traffic and weather and a few fires, Cross's interest perked up when he saw the screen show a picture of Shanahan standing behind Kowalski. Cross hadn't connected Shanahan to the case of the missing girl, but it made sense. She worked for the company that Pedersen ran.

Cross turned up the volume. No new news, just a rehash of the story that now included the press conference and a brief interview with Rafferty. What followed caused Cross to forget about everything else—including Margot. He saw several photographs of Lianna Bailey—as a young girl, at graduation, and as a well-dressed professional adult. What struck Cross was the resemblance of the missing Lianna Bailey and the disappearing platinum-haired dancer.

He tried to call Shanahan, but the line was busy.

Something was up. He knew it. He felt the energy re-ignite his numb brain.

Thirteen

Maureen came into the kitchen with a stack of mail and multicolored flyers for car dealers and supermarkets. "Yesssssss, Mr. Shanahan. You have a secret admirer?" She handed him a letter, personally addressed to "D. Shanahan." In rather awkward printed letters, it also said, "personal." No return address. Maureen looked at him with a Mona Lisa smile, fluttered her eyelashes. "Personal. La De Dah!"

Shanahan opened it. It didn't take long to read. "D, call me from a public phone at this number." There was a phone number and a signature of sorts. "Swann."

Shanahan looked at the postmark. It was sent day before yesterday. This was unlike Swann, a play-by-the-book in all of the best and worst senses of the description. Anything surreptitious was beyond him.

"Is it scented?" Maureen asked when Shanahan looked up.

Shanahan brought the paper to his nose, sniffed. "Hmmmn, I can't tell. It's either Old Spice or Aqua Velva." He waited for her to comment. She waited for him. "It's Swann. Wants a private talk."

"Go," she said, smiling. "I have half a dozen calls to make."

Shanahan stopped at Harry's just as Harry was opening up. They acknowledged each other with a nod. Neither spoke. Shanahan grabbed the phone and dialed. A woman answered.

"Is Swann there?" Shanahan forgot the man's first name. It was always Swann or at best, Lt. Swann.

Swann came on. "I want to talk with you." His voice was dry, fatigued. "Meet you some place."

95

"What time are you off duty?"

"I'm on vacation. Somebody thought I needed the rest," Swann said in flat tones.

"Where should we go and when?"

"Now is a good time," Swann said. "Main Library. You know where the stacks are on the second floor?"

"Yep."

"Meet in mysteries. How about the 'L's for Lianna?"

Shanahan was always able to contain his amusement; but it was difficult seeing Swann, normally a smooth-shaven high-school principal type, looking like Humphrey Bogart in *Desperado*.

Despite the heat outside, it was cool back in the stacks— rows of books unartfully displayed on metal shelves under fluorescent light. This was a far cry from the wonderfully grand lobby, with stairways on each side and huge chandeliers hanging from the high ceilings. Only the serious reader came back in the stacks, which, Shanahan thought, meant few visitors.

"What's all this?" Shanahan asked of Swann, who was looking down into an open book.

"I don't like it, Shanahan," he said. He looked like he'd lost his best friend. Maybe he had.

"I'm all ears."

"No, I mean I don't like talking to you about this."

"You called me down here to tell me you don't want to talk to me?"

"Thing is, I don't like what they're doing more than I don't like what I'm doing talking to you."

"Glad you cleared things up."

Swann was quiet, gathering his thoughts. He either didn't think Shanahan was funny or he didn't care. Shanahan thought the latter. Swann was carrying too much weight to be civil.

"Rafferty is running this homicide investigation," Swann said, looking at Shanahan with the knowledge that the detective knew how pregnant that statement was.

"You complain to the right people?"

"That's why I'm on vacation."

"You going to fill me in?"

"That's why I'm here. But I'm not happy about it."
Swann looked around and continued.

"Your boy may be guilty. I don't know. It looks that way
from here. On the other hand, what Rafferty is doing is not
right. He's acting like a prosecutor, not examining any other
possibilities. I'm not sure whether that's because he knows
nothing about homicide or because he has to manage the case
in order to please higher-ups. No one is allowed to go near
certain people."

"By certain people you mean Pedersen."

Swann nodded.

"Why is that?" Shanahan asked, but he pretty much knew
the answer.

"Because everybody is scared of Pedersen. The Mayor, the
Governor. If he got upset and moved Noah Rose and Company
to New Jersey, there goes one hell of a lot of high-paying
jobs, tax revenue, and an incredible amount of philanthropy.
And it seems that Pedersen is determined that Todd Evans did
it and he wants it wrapped up that way, leaving his company
with as little publicity as possible."

"You didn't want to play along?"

"I can't," Swann said. "I can't. I can't work that way. Maybe
I'd come to the same conclusion, but that's not the way to get
there."

"Can you tell me what you know?"

"I never thought I'd do this."

"Cross the blue line?"

He shook his head, angry that it had come to this.

"If it's any consolation, Rafferty isn't a real cop, you know.
He plays one on TV." Swann wasn't moved. "You want to go
some place, sit down?" Shanahan asked. "We could go over
to Harry's on 10th."

"No, we do it here," Swann said.

"What do you know?"

"Here's how they read it. Todd Evans knew it wasn't his kid. But he waited, let the anger build. He found someone who looked like Lianna, bought her a ticket to San Francisco, then killed his girlfriend."

"That's pretty thin," Shanahan said. "You think somebody like Todd Evans had a mind like that?"

"No, but I don't go by hunches about a guy's character. You'd be surprised what goes on in the world." He looked at Shanahan. "Well, maybe not. But the point is there were no fingerprints on the steering wheel of her car. None on the door handle. Why would Lianna wipe off her fingerprints?"

"You're making Rafferty's case," Shanahan said.

"Yeah, and I wouldn't mind helping Rafferty with the case, but he's made no effort to find out who the other boyfriend is. I mean maybe he didn't want a kid either. Maybe he's married."

"Maybe he's Pedersen," Shanahan said.

"Maybe. Maybe a lot of things. Maybe she was raped and didn't want to lose the kid. Maybe, maybe, maybe. You have to rule these things out. You can't just go full bore after the first person you see."

"It still seems thin."

"He was the last to see her. He acknowledged an argument. He had no alibi for the time she disappeared. The insurance policy. The missing fingerprints. Oh, there are fingerprints on the car. His on the trunk. They found hair and skin particles that suggest she could have spent time in the trunk. Now that they have him under their control, they figure they can break him down."

"You read any of these?" Shanahan asked, gesturing to the row upon row of mystery novels. He wanted to calm the lieutenant.

"No. They'd just piss me off," Swann said smiling. "They always get solved, you know. The bad get punished. That's not the way it is."

"That's supposed to be the goal. We can try for it," Shanahan said. "What now?"

"It's yours. If I find out something, I'll figure out how to get the information to you. But don't count on it." He looked at Shanahan and, seemingly satisfied that he had done all he could do, walked away.

Shanahan found a note stuck to the refrigerator. "Call Howie right away!"
He knew the number by heart and dialed it.
"Cross," said the voice.
"You called?"
"I might have something for you."
"What do you mean?" Shanahan asked cautiously.
"About Lianna Bailey."
"I'll be right over." Shanahan said.
"You don't—"
"You don't mind me dropping by," Shanahan interrupted.
"I'll break out the wine and caviar."

Fourteen

"It didn't dawn on me before," Cross said, leading the way to the living room. He fell into the sofa. "I want in on the investigation."

"I don't think you do," Shanahan said. "Nobody's getting much of anything. Some money has to go to Kowalski . . ."

"Hey, this one is not about the money."

"What's going on?" Shanahan said.

"This morning, they showed half a dozen pictures or so of Lianna, you know, as a kind of retrospective of her life. She bears a resemblance to a dancer at a strip club over on Northwestern."

Shanahan waited a moment. He knew where this was going. This looked like it fit right in with Rafferty's theory. That didn't make him happy.

"And?" he asked as Cross took his time to find the right words.

"She didn't show up for work. Didn't tell anybody. Just didn't show up. Left no forwarding address."

"Comes with the territory. We're not talking about the nursing profession," not believing his own devil's advocacy.

"Roughly the same build. Same face. Same age. She comes up missing the same time Lianna comes up missing. I want to work with you and check it out. My dime."

"Why?" Shanahan asked.

"Settle a score."

"Should I know?"

"We talked about it. Wayward husband stiffs me on a bill."

"And he's connected to the stripper?"

"Some way or other. She goes off with him, doesn't come back. He shows up on my doorstep awful quick. If it was a quickie he was after, they wouldn't have had to leave the club." He looked at Shanahan. "Why are you still standing?"

"Waiting for the Champagne."

"Sorry, my butler is boycotting the French."

"The Italians make sparkling wine, I'm told."

"He's not serving anything with bubbles in it. So don't ask for a Coke either."

"OK, the caviar."

"What's caviar without Champagne? C'mon, let me in on this. Free sidekick."

"What are you thinking?"

"I'm thinking maybe I go back to this guy, Channing, and I drop the name Lianna Bailey and see what happens."

"If you really want in, you're in," Shanahan said, "but let me talk to your friend Channing. Let him think there's more than one person after him. Later, do what you want with him, but let me play the Lianna angle for now."

Cross smiled. "I like it." He took a deep breath. "If we find Norah, we might find out a whole lot more."

Shanahan filled him in on what Swann told him, about Rafferty's theory and about the police lieutenant's doubts.

"The question. Could a young investment analyst figure all this out?" Shanahan asked.

"Yeah, I'm afraid he could. Complete with the amateur touch of wiping off the prints."

"I wish you weren't right. Whatever connections you have left with the IPD could come in handy. Especially with the coroner's office if it comes to that. At this stage, I'll take rumors and speculation. Something else. I can't get to Pedersen. You need to find out what kind of relationship he had with Lianna."

"You're not asking much. How am I supposed to get to the city's leading CEO?" Cross stood, went to the glass doors that led out to a small gravel patio.

"Kowalski might be able to help," Shanahan said.

Cross turned back. "I think I should go to San Francisco."

"Instead of follow the money, it's follow the dancer?"

"Yeah," Cross said. "Should be more fun, don't you think?"

"You're suggesting she might be pretty easy to find."

"She's a good dancer . . ."

"You know about these things, I take it," Shanahan said.

"All too well."

"So you're saying someone has to traipse through all of the strip clubs in a city known for its friendliness to madams."

"She won't be dancing at some dive for dollar bills. There can't be that many high-class clubs."

"The plane ticket took her to San Francisco. Who knows where she ended up. Could be Las Vegas. Whoever sent her doesn't want her found either, right? Who said she stayed in San Francisco? She could have gone on to Honolulu or the Cook Islands."

"Oh God," Cross said, a sick look on his face.

"What?"

"They don't need her anymore. She's a liability. With all this investigating, she can screw up the works."

"Well, Evans isn't going anywhere soon."

"No. Channing's involved and probably not on his own." Cross stood, moved to the wall of windows. "You know if these guys are cold-blooded enough to kill a pregnant woman," Cross said, "why wouldn't they wait until she got to San Francisco, then kill her there? Dump her in some prostitute alley somewhere. Eliminate the witness. Cops in San Francisco, or Vegas for that matter, wouldn't know how to connect the body to Lianna's case."

Cross paced.

"So you really want to go out there?"

"What we need is to get to Channing right away. Right now."

"I'll go. Give me an address," Shanahan said. Cross's mental state seemed a little tender and he didn't want the meeting with Channing to get physical.

Cross went to the room where he had his computer to find a pen and paper.

Shanahan called out after him. "Why don't you do what you can with your friends on the force? Were there any cell phone calls? Charge card fees that we can trace down the dancer?"

Cross came back in, handed Shanahan the address, written on the ripped corner of a yellow pad.

"You sure know how to cut down on expenses," Shanahan said. "And, if you can, try to take a little more philosophical approach to Channing."

"Channing stiffed me $1200," he said, then looked upset or ashamed maybe. "I mean the girl is the most important. But just wanted you to know what kind of guy you're dealing with."

The woman who answered the door seemed frightened. A thin, bony woman with eyes that were both wide open and tired, she kept her hand on the doorknob.

"My name is Shanahan. You are Mrs. Channing?"

"Yes," she said cautiously.

"Is your husband at home?"

"No." Worry continued to gather across her face.

"You and your husband own the house. Is that correct?" Shanahan asked with as pleasant a voice as he could muster.

"Yes. Why?"

"Well, I work for an attorney and we're about to put a lien against your house. Just wanted to verify that this was the correct house."

"What? What are you talking about?"

"That's not for me to say," Shanahan said. He was sorry about scaring her. "I'm sure it's just a misunderstanding."

"You must tell me . . . I'm . . . It's . . ." she stumbled.

"I'm sorry. It has something to do with a check made payable to Howard Cross under false pretenses. There may be some other criminal charges at some point. You signed the check, right?"

"I . . . I'm sorry . . . it's not what I wanted."

"I'm sure you can work this out somehow. You might want to get in touch with a bail bond company."

"Why?"

"To be sure that you don't spend very long in jail."

"I don't understand any of this," she said, genuinely frightened now. "I need to call my husband. Can you wait a moment? Please."

As she turned to go inside, Shanahan followed. When she turned to see him, she looked even more alarmed. Shanahan smiled. She searched the kitchen counter for a piece of paper and then went to a wireless phone, plucked it from its stand. Shanahan angled so he could see her punch in the numbers. He was pretty sure he got the number. The area code was 415. Wasn't a local call.

"Mr. Channing's room, please."

She waited, eyes darting quickly back and forth from Shanahan. No one answered, apparently. She clicked off the phone, set it down.

"He's not there yet," she said as if she just heard that a loved one had died. "What can I do?" she asked.

"I guess you could pay what you owe him and he'll drop all legal action."

She swallowed, looked at the floor as if it would provide an answer. It did. She went to the living room, found her purse, and pulled out a checkbook.

"Get this to the bank right away," Shanahan said to a happily bewildered Cross. "I'm not sure how long it will take for your friend to stop payment."

"How'd you do that?" Cross said, stepping aside so Shanahan could step inside.

"Not sure if it's good. Maybe, she might have just wanted to get rid of me. Go to the bank. Get the cash before they stop it."

"And you?"

"I'm going to San Francisco."

"You know who you're looking for?"

"Channing. I know where he's staying."

"I gotta go," Cross said.

"There goes your $1200."

"And then some," Cross said.

"Problem is he's already on his way or maybe he's landed. As of ten minutes ago, he hadn't checked into the hotel. We may be too late."

"I have an idea," Cross said, picking up his phone. "I know a guy out there." He dialed. "What's the name of the hotel?" he asked Shanahan.

"The Grant Hotel."

"Nick, this is Cross in Indianapolis." There was quiet. "I'll call later to catch up, but I have something urgent. You have to trust me." Cross listened. "There's one hundred in it just for delivering a simple message. In person." Cross was quiet. "I know, I know, but it's got to be this way. Right now, you go to the Grant Hotel. Speak to Lester Channing. Tell him to go home. No questions. No phone calls. Tell him not to do anything. He's being watched and for him to go back to Indianapolis. That's it. Don't answer questions." More quiet. "Now listen, Nick, Channing is an ex-cop and dangerous. Carry protection." Another moment of Cross listening. "No, not a condom," Cross laughed. "You never change. If he's not there find him or wait for him. I'll pay extra. He's got to get the message as soon as possible." Cross waited, now impatiently. "Don't have time. Go now. I'll fill you in later."

"Anything from your friends at IPD?" Shanahan asked as he headed for the door.

"I was just trying to check in when you came back. I'm on it."

What Shanahan knew before he told Maureen that he was planning to go a place known for having the finest food in the country was that she would want to join him. When he explained that he might be spending a good deal of his time in strip clubs, she simply bought the tickets.

Maureen felt guilty feeling good. She knew that Shanahan thought that the girl he was looking for was in danger of her

life, but half her mind was already daydreaming about hills
and Italian restaurants.

"You can't just call the police out there?" Maureen asked.

"We did something like that," Shanahan said.

"American Trans Air," she said. "Six A.M."

Cross wished he were a fly on the wall when his friend
Nicholas Lang talked to Lester Channing. At some point
he'd make sure Channing knew what was done to him, and
by whom. Cross definitely wanted the credit. For now, he
thought this just might work. He doubted that Channing was
working on his own. Maybe Shanahan was right. Maybe
Pedersen had something to do with all of this. Though it
could be Evans.

Cross stayed up all night. He'd sleep on the plane.

It was four fifteen in the morning when Cross found two taxi
cabs waiting in front of his home. At first he thought there
was some sort of error with the dispatcher, but he saw Margot
get out of the second one. She looked at him, noticed the suitcase.

"Stay with me," she said.

"I can't," he said. He moved quickly toward the other cab,
hoping he could get in, escape before she wore him down.
She had that talent.

"You have to. I need you," she said.

He opened the back door to the taxi, tossing in his suitcase.
He reached in his pocket, tossed her the keys. "Go in, sleep.
I'll call you."

She caught them. "Where are you going?"

"Away," he said, wanting to leave it at that. What right did
she have to personal information? She gave none. Everything,
all the time, was on her terms. He couldn't be as hard as he
wanted to. "For a few days."

"That important, is it?"

"Yes. That important."

"A girl?"

"A case." It was a girl, sort of. If he hadn't committed to Shanahan, he might not be able to leave.

"I'm frightened."

"Get used to it. We all are." There. Something firm. A firm admission that he was frightened too. It came out naturally. He was glad for a second. Then he was sorry. He got into the taxi and told the driver where he needed to go.

"Wait." She was at the window. She pulled a manila envelope from her handbag. He rolled down the window. "Here," she said. "Here's your little platinum canary. The club didn't need it anymore." She smiled, turned.

He waited awhile before he looked back. Margot was climbing the steps. The taxi pulled away.

Cross was so sorry. So sorry for everything. Everyone. Including himself.

Fifteen

Shanahan and Maureen sat patiently. Maureen read a copy of *USA Today* that had been casually tossed on one of the seats.

"I don't think anybody reads that unless they're at the airport," Cross said, arriving with his carryon. "It's like fruitcake, they only make one and people pass it around. Do I have time for coffee?"

"I'll join you," Shanahan said. "You find anything?"

"There was a cell phone call after the time Lianna would have arrived in San Francisco. But you aren't going to like who the call went to."

"Who?" He was pretty sure he knew the answer.

"Todd Evans."

"What does that prove?" Shanahan asked defensively. Maybe it didn't prove anything, but it suggested some things that would bring more glee to the prosecution than to Kowalski.

"It was a call of confirmation. 'I made it safely to San Francisco. I did my part. Bye now.' Don't you think?"

Shanahan took a deep breath, ordered his coffee black. He couldn't see a situation in which a call like that would be helpful. Little by not so little, the police were building a very, very good circumstantial case against Evans.

"Something else," Cross said. "My friend Nick got to the hotel and was waiting in the lobby when Channing arrived. Channing said nothing when he was told to go home. Nothing. I mean, you'd think his first reaction would be, 'Who the hell are you?' or 'I don't know what the hell you're talking about.' Nothing. Didn't volunteer anything."

"The bluff worked, maybe," Shanahan said. "That probably means he's working for somebody. He's taking orders."

"That's speculation," Cross said.

"That's why I used the word, 'probably.'"

"And you're thinking the guy he's working for is Pedersen?"

"If you hire a hit, you have to pay for it," Shanahan said. "Evans could have had a few bucks stashed away somewhere."

"And the means to find someone to do it."

"Just Pedersen, only Pedersen. Isn't this as bad as the cops only going after Todd?"

"Yeah," Shanahan said, "let's balance the accusations. But having all that cop in your blood, you're thinking it could still be young Todd?"

Cross nodded. "Could be. People have hired killers before, especially if they didn't have what it takes to actually do it."

"No, that's completely premeditated," Shanahan said, blowing on his steaming coffee to cool it a bit. "You might convince me that they had an argument and Todd went too far, but—"

"Hey, I'm sure your instincts about character are pretty good. On the other hand mass murderers have been known to be big-eyed, innocent, charming and good looking guys."

"Who is charming and good looking?" Maureen asked, overhearing the conversation as they returned to the gate.

"Lady-killers," Shanahan said.

"And you don't mean that in a good way, I take it?" she asked.

Because the jet flew with the sun, it was still morning when the three of them landed in San Francisco International Airport. Shanahan knew there were larger airports and larger cities, but compared to Indianapolis, both seemed immense. On the taxi ride into the city, the whitish silver skyline was expansive though the tips of the tallest buildings were hidden in fog. It was a quiet ride despite the attempts of the Mid-Eastern driver to liven up his passengers. In the city, the activity on

the streets made Indianapolis look like a ghost town, a pleasant ghost town, but a city of relatively quiet, unpopulated
streets.

Maureen had booked them two rooms in a small, modestly
priced—for San Francisco that is—hotel. It was a couple of
blocks west of Union Square in a neighborhood that seemed
like the poor cousin of Nob Hill, just a short, but steep climb
away.

"What do we do now?" Cross said as he headed toward his
room next door.

"I say we eat," Maureen said. Glancing at the look on
Shanahan's face, she smiled. "I know, I know. We're here on
business. But we have to keep up our strength."

"Let's plan on a nice dinner, but we need to figure out how
we're going to do this."

"Do what?" Cross said.

"Exactly," Shanahan replied.

Cross checked the *Yellow Pages* and couldn't make heads or
tails of the listings. He checked nightclubs, adult entertainment, strippers. Nothing clued him in. He went to the lobby,
picked up a newspaper and was disappointed to find there
were only a few clubs listed near the movie section.

He pulled Nick's phone number from his pocket and
punched in the numbers.

"Nick, another favor?"

"Let me tell you about the first one," Nick said. "I waited
outside the hotel to see if your guy would grab a cab back to
the airport. You know, he hadn't even checked in when I talked
to him."

"What happened?"

"He came out without baggage, started walking."

"And?"

He walked to an apartment building in the Tenderloin, rang
a buzzer for way too long, walked to a bar called a Summer
Place. Troy Donahue wasn't there. I eventually gave up, didn't
know what to do, couldn't get in touch with you."

"Thanks. This isn't good news."

"I didn't figure it was. Maybe he couldn't get a plane last night and thought what the hell, he'd just stay and enjoy himself. Thing is he didn't look like he was enjoying himself."

"Nick, what I need is a list of the nice strip clubs in town."

"You mean gentleman's clubs?" Nick laughed.

"I guess. I can't imagine Norah working at some meat rack. Maybe something with class."

"OK, probably she's at one of the topless clubs rather than the nude clubs."

"Let me in on this. Why would there be topless clubs if full nudity was legal?"

"At the topless clubs, they serve alcohol. Hell, some of them serve fine dinners."

"OK. You know them?"

"Can't afford them, but yeah, there's just a few of them. Larry Flynt's got a place here on Kearny. The Gold Club is South of Market. There's a couple up on Broadway."

"Open in the afternoon?"

"Yeah. Good time to go. Low cover. Cheap drinks. You want to go? I'll meet you. You owe me a drink."

"Or twenty."

It was still early afternoon when Cross went on his tour of gentleman's clubs. Maureen encouraged Shanahan to go along. In fact, she wanted to go along, but in the interest of expense and time, Shanahan begged off. Instead Cross left him a list of the people who served on the board of directors of Mason Life Systems, Pedersen's old company. Some of them were presidents or CEOs of companies in San Francisco.

What were the chances that Shanahan could talk with them? Better than average if it was true Pedersen wasn't all that well liked.

On the fifth call, he was connected with one of the names, but was dismissed quickly when Shanahan started asking questions.

On the thirteenth call, Shanahan struck gold. Emile Morales

wanted to talk. The phone wouldn't do though. Could Shanahan meet him at Café Claude's? It was a little restaurant in an alley just off Bush, halfway between Marino's offices and Shanahan's hotel.

"Definitely walkable," the desk clerk said. "No hills between here and there."

Maureen veered off as they passed near Union Square.

"I want to go gawk at Gucci's," she said.

The fog had burned off and Shanahan had worked up a mild sweat. Maybe there were no hills, but it wasn't exactly flat either and the older detective walked quickly. He didn't want to chance being late.

Emile was in his sixties, slender, good looking, sitting at a table under an umbrella in the brick alleyway. There were shops further on. Like most people who first met Shanahan, there was a moment of shock or disbelief. Morales recovered quickly and offered his hand. There was a quarter of an inch of white cuff at the edge of Morales's shirtsleeve. A handsome, surprisingly simple Rolex on his wrist. His fingernails were manicured and painted a clear matte. His teeth were nearly as white as Pedersen's. He smiled. They both sat.

The waiter had a thick French accent. Shanahan wondered if it were real. He guessed it was.

"So you are not a fan of Bradley Gray Pedersen?" Emile asked after the waiter arrived, handed them menus and departed. Morales's eyes were full of humor, maybe mischief.

"No. I asked an indiscreet question or two and found myself dealing with a restraining order."

"One of his many weapons," Morales said. "What has he done?"

"He's not helping a murder investigation in which he might or might not have played a part."

Morales looked disappointed.

"I would seriously doubt that, Mr. Shanahan. He's quite capable of doing worse, but doing something so mundane and personal as murder? No." Morales's voice trailed off. He shook his head. "No."

"Did he have a weakness for young women?"

"Who doesn't? What he had was a big, big vision and a bigger ego. He thought the sun rose and set for him and if you didn't agree, you weren't part of his universe. Murder? No. As I said, he was capable of much larger crimes."

"A little past reading of Mason Life Systems press reports suggests that he wasn't well-liked by the firm he nearly owned."

"Nearly is the operative word," Morales said. "I'd like for you to stand up a moment, Mr. Shanahan. Take off your jacket, and open your shirt."

"What?"

"We're going to have a nice chat. It may help you. It may not. But when it's over, we will enter a little time machine, and we'll come back and redo it. We won't have talked. I would have mistakenly thought we were meeting at the little French restaurant in Belden Alley. We would have just missed each other by a few blocks. And you will know only what you've dreamed."

"Very colorful," Shanahan said. He stood, did what he was told to do, then sat down to listen to the story.

Nick suggested what he described as a nice club in North Beach. The cab climbed up the hill and dropped Cross off in front. The entrance was down a few steps. He was greeted at the door by a handsome fellow in a dark suit.

"You've been here before," he said more as a statement than a question. Cross didn't correct him. He didn't want the sales pitch. The slender Asian woman behind a counter traded her five for Cross's ten.

"I'm André," the fellow said, "watch your step." Cross took another step down and into the darkened room. "The bar?"

"Yes. Just the bar," Cross said, noticing he was now the only customer.

"Lilly is the bartender."

Cross went to the bar without further escort, noticing there were half a dozen girls sitting in plush chairs around various tables. The stage was in a pit and there in the brightest light in the room was a blonde. She danced topless, her flesh as pale as a new moon.

Cross ordered a Scotch from Lilly, who seemed pretty neutral about her only customer. He ordered Scotch because it was something he could nurse or drink up, depending on the need.

Seemingly out of nowhere, a cute young dancer, top and bottom covered, though barely, wanted to chat. She set a little box on the bar. It was pink, had a handle like a purse, and a slot for tips.

"How's your day going?" she asked.

Cross wanted to help her out. She was having a slow day, but money would be encouragement.

"I hope your day's going pretty well. Maybe we'll talk later."

"I'll be over there when you're ready," she said, nodding to the nearest table.

"Excuse me," he said to Lilly, the bartender. "Could you help me?" She came over cautiously, noticing that he'd put an 8 by 10 photograph on the bar, under one of the soft lights.

"Hey Cross!" It was Nick. He moved in beside Cross.

"You two brothers?" Lilly asked, suddenly interested. Perhaps she was interested in Nick. Maybe she knew him.

"Cousins seven times removed," Nick said.

"You look like you were separated at birth," Lilly said. "You're not cops or you would have flashed your badges."

"Here," Nick said, opening his wallet, showing his ID.

"Doesn't matter. Don't know her. Girls here don't usually get all dolled up in feathers and glitter."

"Beer. Anything foreign," Nick told her. "So," he said looking at the photograph, "a lost angel."

"Could be in trouble."

"Sorry about not keeping on top of your Channing character."

"He may be out here to kill the angel."

They talked, but not for long. Nick had an appointment at two thirty and Howie had half a dozen gentleman's clubs to go.

Outside, Nick grabbed Howie's shoulder.

"My friend. A little orientation." They stood outside the bar, halfway up the hill on Kearny. "Behind us is Chinatown," he pointed. "South is the financial district. They have banks from countries I've never heard of. Over there is Jackson Square, the neighborhood for high-end antiques."

"I don't need that," Cross said. "I am a low-end kind of guy."

"And further up the hill is Broadway. Lots of flesh joints right and left. Roaring 20s, Lusty Ladies, Little Darlings. The Hungry I used to be where Lenny Bruce and Mort Sahl did their comedy. Now it's a strip club. Most of the Broadway clubs, you don't come close to getting what you pay for. But you might want to check them out while you're here. I gotta go earn a living, that is if you call this a living." Nick laughed, hit Cross on the shoulder. "Good luck, man. Call me if you need anything."

Cross hiked up the hill, onto Broadway, a tawdry collection of neon that probably looked more appealingly lurid at night. He picked the first strip club he saw. Behind the bar was a woman with an ample bosom who apparently hadn't the fabric to cover it all. Cross tried to smile pleasantly; but wasn't sure he was carrying it off.

"Have you seen her?" Cross asked, after flashing the 8 by 10.

"If I did why would I tell you?"

The smile didn't work.

"Tip, maybe?" He put a ten on the bar.

"I don't know you. If I knew her why would I tell some stranger where she was?"

"She's in danger," Cross said.

"Now, let me guess from who. Stalking has become a national sport, or haven't you been reading the papers?"

Cross pulled out his wallet, showed his ID. Too much Jerry Springer, he thought. She looked at the wallet, took it from him, held it under the light by the cash register.

"A long way from home. Indiana, huh?"

"Land of Lincoln, despite what Illinois says. Lots of corn too."

"David Letterman," she added. "That makes you a Hoosier, right?"

"Yeah, I guess it does. Just a countrified Hoosier in the big city, trying to help some lady stay alive. Lots of places to go, people to see. Think you can help?"

"Oh . . . crap," she said, giving in. "I haven't seen anyone looks like her. Sorry."

She took the ten, looked at Cross, gave him a half smile, and shrugged. "It's been slow," she said.

Sixteen

Cross, having hit the clubs in North Beach, checked out the few in the Tenderloin, and some on Market. Nothing. The club owners, bartenders, and waitresses he talked to were certain they hadn't seen her.

It was exhausting, not to mention demoralizing. What made it worse was that the places were nearly empty. Lots of girls standing around, losing money.

He took a taxi to the Gold Club, in an area called SOMA, South of Market, an old industrial neighborhood, more recently a dot-com haven, and now in the midst of an as yet unidentified transformation. The Club was a nice place, as these places go and the last one on his list. One of the girls was kind enough to put an end to Cross's misery, a period on the sentence that said he was traveling the wrong road.

Cross called the hotel and asked for Shanahan's room, reported his failure to pick up her trail.

"I may have something," Shanahan said, "but it won't help us find the dancer."

After much discussion, they decided to find a place to eat and reorder their thoughts.

"We could eat here at the Gold Club," Cross said. "Quite a menu. No innuendo. A real menu. Delmonico steak. Porterhouse."

"You think you can get a great cup of coffee in a laundromat?" Shanahan said.

Maybe you could, maybe you couldn't. At the moment, Cross really didn't care.

* * *

While Maureen made the arrangements and got ready for her San Francisco dinner, Cross and Shanahan went to the apartment house that Nick mentioned—the one Channing visited after leaving his hotel.

No familiar names on the mail boxes. Nothing hinting at a Norah or an Elizabeth Jefferson. They buzzed the manager. It took him awhile to come to the door and it was apparent he wasn't using that time to freshen up.

Cross showed him the photograph.

"Gone with the wind," the man said. He had more than a five o'clock shadow and a look that daylong drinking will give a guy.

"When?"

"Yesterday, maybe day before yesterday. Time's a bummer."

"Where did she go?"

"NFA," he said.

"No forwarding address?" Cross asked.

"Astute," the man said.

"She seem in a rush?" Shanahan asked.

"She still had until the end of May. She didn't ask for a refund."

"Would she have gotten it?" Cross asked.

"Of course not, but people usually ask."

"She leave anything behind?"

"What's with you guys. Is this some initiation or something?"

"What?" Cross asked.

"Guy yesterday asking the same questions."

"What did you tell him?"

"Same thing I'm telling you."

"You and her talk much?" Cross asked.

"No." He started to shut the door. Cross pressed his hand against it.

"She have visitors?"

"Some black dudes in suits once."

"Friends of hers or business maybe?" Shanahan asked.

"They were laughing. Chilled. They went upstairs."

118

"How do you know?" Cross asked. They had the poor guy in a crossfire.

"Got a call from a neighbor. Music too loud. I talked to them, they're cool. No problem."

"What name did she go by?" Shanahan asked.

"You asking all these questions and you don't know her name?" he asked, eyebrows furrowing. He started to retreat and the open door narrowed. Cross pressed his hand against it again, preventing the man's escape.

"She had a couple of names," Cross said. "We're just trying to figure out which one she's using now." Cross pulled a twenty from his pocket.

"Nina Moore," the man said, seemingly surprised at his memory.

"The guy who was here yesterday. Did you tell him all of this?" Shanahan asked.

"Maybe. I don't know. We talked. I didn't memorize the conversation."

"Shit," Cross said, echoing Shanahan's sentiments. The elder PI figured the man was telling the truth. Then, as now, the man's brain was soggy from a little too much cheap wine.

"I gotta get back now," the man said, closing the door.

The sky turned gray before the sun went down. Dampness crept into the air as the two private investigators flagged a Luxor taxi and headed for Zuni's on Market Street, where, if things went as planned, Maureen would be waiting.

"Our little bluff didn't work with Channing," Cross said. "But he couldn't find her either."

"Question is who will find her first."

Zuni's was bustling. Lots of chatter and clatter. The restaurant was wider than deep, big windows stretching along Market Street. The copper-plated bar was in the entry room and was packed, mostly with wine drinkers. There was a piano and the room tinkled with keys and glasses. Maureen, dressed simply in black, held a glass of red wine in her hand as she chatted with two plump, balding, sixty-ish gentlemen, a younger, more

119

fit Caucasian with more hair and a younger, slenderer Asian. It took her a moment to excuse herself.

"One of them is having a birthday," Maureen said, sidling up to the new arrivals.

"And I didn't bring a gift," Cross said.

"They're running behind," Maureen said, nodding toward the restaurant. "Twenty minutes at least. Can I get you something? This Zinfandel is pretty good."

"I yield to the gentle woman of Indiana," Cross said. "Whatever is fine."

"Me too," Shanahan said. It was her night. On the other hand, he felt a little out of place. His clothes were probably at least a decade off. If there were a third hand, he'd have to admit he loved the smells. Loved seeing Maureen enjoy herself. She wasn't putting on airs, she was simply absorbing the sensuous atmosphere.

She handed Shanahan her wine glass and went back to the bar.

"Nice place," Cross said.

Shanahan nodded. "A lot like Harry's, don't you think?" She exchanged a few more words with the odd trio she talked with before as she waited for her order.

"Then I won't be getting the stew," Cross said.

They sat a table away from the expansive walls of windows. There was a warm, golden light inside. Outside, the fog had muted the early evening's dim remainder of the day. Lampposts were lit, but the light dispersed fuzzily in the moist air. Faint, almost ghost-like streetcars moved slowly across the tintype screen of Shanahan's vision. Where was he? In what time was he living?

He looked at Maureen bathed in gold. She never looked more beautiful. Was it the wine? Was it some chemical dance in his brain? He felt warm, blessed in a magical time and place.

"I'm feeling like a fifth wheel," Cross said.

"Third, just a third wheel," Shanahan said, coming marginally back to the moment.

Roasted chicken, garlic fries, a change in wine, from red to white.

The painting above the doorway showed a woman in a slip, alone and lonely in what appeared to be a bedroom.

"We can't find her," Shanahan said to Maureen.

"Not at any of the clubs. No one's seen her." Cross tore off a piece of sourdough.

"If I were given some money and told to come to San Francisco, the first thing I wouldn't do is get a job, especially if that job was stripping," she said. "You know, Howie, you mentioned that she didn't really like dancing . . ."

"She wanted to become a singer," Howie said. "God, could it have been any more obvious? She's changed her name to Nina Moore."

"Nina Moore is a singer's name, not a stripper's name, seems to me," Maureen said. "And if I had a life I didn't like and someone came along to offer me a way out," she looked at Shanahan, "I'd take it. I did, you know."

"We've been looking in all the wrong places."

"You suppose Channing has that figured out as well?" Shanahan asked.

"Don't know. But this . . . friend of mine," Cross said, wanting to avoid talking about Margot, thinking about Margot, "thought she was into jazz and blues. Not pop," Cross said. He shook his head, not only thinking about his questions, but also trying to dismiss his mind drift toward Margot. "How many places in this city would someone like our little canary go to find a gig?"

"Are you having a good time?" Maureen asked Shanahan when Cross stepped outside to make a phone call.

"Yes. The food is wonderful. I'm enjoying the wine, the restaurant, and you."

"But now you are all bothered again?"

"Yes," Shanahan said. "I feel like I'm fiddling while Nina Moore burns. Channing's going to kill her. She knows too much. She knows who is involved in the crime."

"Maybe they're lovers, Channing and Nina Moore."

"If they were, he'd know where she was. He wouldn't be looking for her."

Cross came back, shrugging off the cold. "If you don't like the weather here, wait a minute," he said, reaching for his napkin to wipe off the moisture on his face. Afterward, he poured himself a little more wine. "My friend Nick is making some calls. He follows the blues scene here. It's not all that big in the city, he says, so maybe we can locate her or where she might go. Then again, there's all of Oakland and who knows where else."

"The guys who came to see her at the apartment house were musicians, I bet," Shanahan said. "They were playing the music too loud. Maybe she was auditioning."

"Or they were just jamming," Maureen said. "I never get to say 'jam,' so I'm happy."

"We'll see," Cross said, finishing off the ounce or so wine in his glass in one gulp. "I think I'll cut down on this. Have a little coffee, get my brain straight. How did your little French café lunch go?"

"Lunch? Lunch? It was lunch?" Maureen asked with mock hysteria.

"Seems Pedersen is a cad among other things," Shanahan said. "Didn't you have lunch?"

"I ate in Macy's basement. And you ate at a French café?"

"You said, 'among other things.' What other things?" Cross asked.

"I want to sift through what he told me," Shanahan said.

"Either he told you squat or it is hot," Cross said, amused at his unintentional rhyme. "I could go into law, what do you think?"

"Or write greeting cards," Shanahan said. "Weird ones."

"What did he say?" Cross insisted. "You can't hold out. That's not fair."

"He made the company uncomfortable with some research he was doing that he refused to share with his board. He had a budget and some very loyal employees, but there was a little room, very secure, that was off-limits to all but a select few. Among the few Lianna Bailey and Mary Beth Schmidt."

"Let's take the streetcar up to Powell," Maureen said. "We can walk to the hotel."

The wind swept through the streets. It was cold, bitter cold. Just a few hours ago Shanahan had worked up a sweat walking to Café Claude. Now he was freezing.

"We might not be done yet," Shanahan said, thinking that Nina Moore was out there somewhere and so was Channing. He had some pieces to this strange puzzle. What Emile Morales told him added a significant piece. It meant more than what he shared with Cross. But what he knew didn't fit anywhere.

They waited for ten minutes on the island in the middle of Market Street. An orange, wooden streetcar rattled to a stop in front of them. It was named "Milan," and it dawned on Shanahan that probably it was from Milan. An antique streetcar. How quaint, he thought. Corny maybe, but he liked it. It added to these oddly timeless moments.

Bicycles, motor scooters, busses, pedestrians, streetcars would appear and disappear in the fog. Yet, the city buzzed even in the cold, gold gauzy night.

A six-year-old boy asked his mother in a voice loud enough for a dozen or so passengers to hear, "Tell me about your most disgusting emergency."

She smiled through her blush and ignored him.

Cross, who was huddling in the back in the corner, answered his phone. He looked up at Shanahan and Maureen, nodded. He talked some more. He flipped his cell phone shut and walked up front.

"We're going in the wrong direction," Cross said.

"Literally or figuratively?" Maureen asked.

"Literally. Figuratively," Cross said, "we're doing OK."

The taxi let the three of them off on the southwest corner of Geary Boulevard and Fillmore Street. A half dozen guys milled about outside smoking. The sign over the door said "John Lee Hooker's Boom Boom Room." Blues met them at the door.

Nick had not only come up with a list of bars where a newcomer might get a chance to break in, but also was able to find where Nina Moore was playing tonight. She had hit the big time right away—she was a guest singer for the Alleytropes for the first set the last few days. She was good. Word of mouth spread quickly to those who followed these things. Likely as not, the only thing she got out of it was exposure, an introduction to those who cared about these things. And, according to Nick's friends, that was all she needed. She set the place on fire.

Inside, the bar stretched down the right wall, one row of tables and chairs down the left. At the far end was the small stage. In between was standing room only, and even that was sparse.

Maureen angled to the bar, ordered drinks, asked questions.

Cross looked around for Channing. The place wasn't big but it was dark and so crowded it was hard to see everybody. Maybe they had been lucky. Maybe they were going to get to her first. She could tell them what she knew and they could warn her about what might happen to her.

"You see Channing anywhere?" Shanahan asked.

"No, but that doesn't mean he's not here. Big white guy, probably will look out of place."

Maureen came back with drinks. "Your personal waitress," she said. "You do tip well, don't you?" After handing out the drinks, she sipped her own rum and tonic. "I told them light on the tonic. I don't think they heard me. Bartender said, she'd be on in a few minutes. The band warms up. She comes on for three songs. Then it's over until tomorrow."

"You need to get up front," Shanahan told Cross. "See if it's the right girl. Maureen, why don't you go up with him? If he gets tied up, you can talk to Nina."

"And you?" Maureen asked.

"I'll watch the door in case the door needs watching."

"He doesn't like crowds," Maureen said to Howie. "A touch of claustrophobia."

At first Howie couldn't tell about the singer. She stood in the spotlight, but her back was to the audience. Then came the voice. Beautiful. She turned. Beautiful. The only thing platinum now was her gown, low cut, tight at the waist and hips, and flaring open to reveal her fantastic legs. The voice of an Etta James and the look of a real vamp from Savannah.

Maureen led Cross further forward, but he stopped suddenly. There, at the table nearest the stage was Channing. He sat with some people that, judging by the body language, he probably didn't know. If Nina Moore knew Channing was there, she didn't show it. Maybe the lights were too bright. Maybe she didn't know enough to be frightened. Maybe she wasn't in danger after all.

"It's her," Cross told Maureen, "and that's him."

Seventeen

Shanahan's energy started to flag. It was only nine thirty in San Francisco, but he was on Midwest time. It was much later. Shanahan went outside, looked around. Other than a few smokers—the club itself was free of smoke, unheard of in Indy bars—outside was quiet, damp, cold. Cars with window wipers, tires on damp streets, streamed by Geary. Whoosh, whoosh, whoosh. There was a line of folks huddled near the bus stop.

Headlights and taillights bounced off the wet streets, as did the light from the neon signs. The Boom Boom Room was on the end of a block and the backend of the building butted up against another. He walked along the wall. There had to be a second door, and there painted into the mural on the wall, was the side door. He'd hang out there.

The light was on Nina Moore, glittering off her gown, flickering in her eyes. She was good, Cross thought. She was into her second song; sensuous elongated vowel sounds purred "Yoooooove Chaaaaanged." Cross had a song and a half to figure out what to do.

Channing was tapping his fingers, but he wasn't on beat. Impatience. Eager to get on with it. Nothing would go on here, but it was likely that the former Cincinnati cop would either force or cajole Nina Moore to go somewhere she would regret going.

"Let me see if I can stop Channing," Cross said as he leaned over to whisper in Maureen's ear. "You follow Nina Moore offstage and see if you can talk with her." Maureen nodded. "Tell her you represent a record label or something," Cross continued. "Then if you get her away from the danger, let her know what's going on."

As Nina brought the second song to a close, she saw Channing. Cross watched her closely. She registered recognition. He couldn't make out anything more. No fear, no happiness. Not even surprise. What was it? Cross asked himself. Was she just completely unaware the role she played? Did she know anything other than she got a free ticket to ride? Maybe she was in on it all. An accomplice. Another possibility, Nina and Channing were lovers—Oh God, he hoped not—and she either knew what was going on or didn't, thinking that Channing was merely being generous.

Nina moved easily from one song to the other, but surprising Cross. She was doing a jazz rendition of Pink Floyd's "San Tropez." "Eatin' a peach" in that slow, slow rhythm that nearly hypnotized the detective. Anyone whose soul moved at that speed was a deeply kindred spirit. That lazy, taking-it-all-in spirit was a match for the secret Cross.

It was a short song and it was over before Cross could get his wits about him. Those who weren't already standing stood, applauding heartily. That included Channing, who, applauding politely and distantly, inadvertently blocked Maureen before she could move in to intercept Nina. The two collided, she curled around his big frame, and once she was past him, Channing started to follow.

"Hey, Channing," Cross said, touching his shoulder.

Channing turned. His face showed bewilderment, surprise and anger, all in a split second.

"What the fuck . . ."

"What in the hell are the chances?" Cross said, shaking his head, as if he were amazed at the idea he'd see Channing there.

Channing turned, noticing Maureen guiding a puzzled Nina backstage. Cross could hear Maureen saying something about a recording contract.

Channing turned back, looking seriously at Cross, trying

desperately to figure out the connection or deliberating on a course of action.

"Can I buy you a drink old buddy?" Cross asked.

"You son of a bitch," he said and moved away from Cross in the direction Maureen and Nina had gone. Cross followed, but the other band members descended from the stage. Channing squeezed through them. The wall closed in front of Cross.

He felt a moment of panic. Maureen and Nina with Channing. He turned back to search for Shanahan. Lots of folks, taking their seats again, milling about, none of them Shanahan.

The side doors burst open. Shanahan saw Maureen pulling Nina out the door, with Channing stumbling after them. Nina looked confused, frightened. Shanahan didn't know if she were afraid of Channing or of Maureen, who now looked at Shanahan as he stepped between them.

"Excuse me sir, do you know where Fillmore Street is?" He barely slowed the big man. Shanahan stepped aside, but left his foot in the way. Channing went down like a rhinoceros.

Maureen waved at a cab, but it evaporated into the fog. The rhino stirred. He struggled to his feet, looking angrily at Shanahan. He had put two and one together. He knew Shanahan was part of it.

Maureen pulled a 9 m.m. from her coat pocket. She aimed it at Channing.

"Did you happen to lose this?" she asked.

Cross came through the doors. He came to a sudden, almost cartoon stop, then took a moment to assess the situation. Everything seemed askew. The gun in Maureen's hand seemed to be the most startling.

"Is this your little party?" Channing said to Cross.

"I just thought we should all spend more time together," Cross said.

"Who are you with, kid?" Channing asked Nina.

"I . . . I . . . don't know."

"I think you're being kidnapped, honey," he said, looking around. Composure regained, he smiled.

"She's free to go," Shanahan said, "as long as she understands about Lianna. There are murder charges, you know?"

Nina looked at Channing.

"Why are you here?" she asked.

"Thought maybe you needed a little more help." He waited for her to understand. She was quiet, expressionless. "You know? Takes money to get a career started. I just wanted you to know the well ain't dry." He nodded toward her in a way that implied understanding, maybe intimacy.

"This isn't going the way . . ." she began. It was as if she just realized there were others present.

"I think Nina here might want to know that if she continues to work with you she'll be an accomplice to your crime. Her look-alike all disappeared and presumed dead. The cops think so."

Channing smiled. "Shit happens," he said. "Some folks win the lottery. Other folks die, you know. That's life."

"And death," Cross said, looking at Nina. "Of course sometimes you get a choice."

"I'm leaving," she said. She looked at Channing. "Alone. Don't call me. I'll call you." Her voice was firm. She walked away.

"You're done," Cross said to Channing.

Channing smirked, held out his hand for the pistol.

"You have to be kidding," Maureen said. She handed it to Shanahan, who pulled out the clip, handed it over to Channing.

"How'd you get that on the plane?" Cross asked.

Channing didn't answer. He put his pistol in the holster. He turned, walked toward the corner.

"We're going to let him go?" Maureen asked.

"Too complicated out here. We'll have to get him back in Indianapolis and just hope Nina stays out of his way."

"He's going to have a hard time getting to the airport," she said.

"Why is that?"

She pulled his wallet out of her other pocket.

"Where did you learn to do that?" Cross asked.

"Her past is sealed. Not even a court order," Shanahan said, taking the wallet, looking inside, pulling out various cards. He couldn't read them in the dim light. He walked under a street lamp.

"Channing's forty-two, born in November, 6'1", 260." He sorted through the other cards. "Video club membership, dentist's appointment card, Chevron charge card . . . hmmm . . . the Blue Moon Sauna and Massage Parlor, with nine out of ten boxes initialed."

"Frequent feeler card, one massage shy of a freebee," Cross said, laughing.

"Covington, Kentucky," Shanahan said.

"Let's go back to the hotel," Maureen said. "It's cold out here."

They walked up to Fillmore. A number of cabs went by, all occupied, before a red one pulled up. On the side of the door was "Big Dog Cab."

"Very colorful," Shanahan said.

It was warm but crowded in the small room. They had been quiet in the taxi and no one seemed to have anything to say.

"What next?" Cross said.

"I don't know if we screwed up or not," Shanahan said. "Not sure there was anything else we could do. Couldn't arrest him. Couldn't hold her."

"She's been warned," Cross said, glancing at Maureen.

"I told her," Maureen said. "She could have held a full house or ten high. I couldn't tell whether she knew what she was participating in or not. All she said was: 'We had a deal and I wasn't supposed to see him again.'"

"What have we got to take back?" Cross said.

"A validation for us, but nothing for the cops," Shanahan said. He pulled out Channing's wallet again. There was a sheet of paper inside with a dozen or so phone numbers. Maybe, Shanahan thought. Maybe that would tell them something.

"We go back tomorrow?" Cross asked.

"We pay extra. We have the rooms one more night and we're scheduled to fly out of here day after tomorrow."

"Enjoy!" Cross said, thinking that he was in one of the world's most desirable cities, and he was stone-cold broke. What did that matter? He knew if he stopped to take a measure of his mood, he'd discover there wasn't anything here, or anywhere, that he wanted. He was nursing something perhaps just shy of serious depression. He went to his room.

"I didn't know you could pick pockets," Shanahan said.

"You might have thought I was at the bottom when I met you, Mr. Shanahan. You would be wrong. I was already on my way up."

"Well, good work," he said, kissing her cheek. "Every time I think I know you, I am equally surprised and impressed. We should mail this to him tomorrow." Shanahan held the wallet in his hand. "After we copy these phone numbers."

Later, the two of them walked out in the cold wet night and down to Union Square. In the bar in the St. Francis, they nursed drinks and watched the crowd, Maureen making up stories about the more interesting ones.

"Do you think we should have invited Howie along?" Maureen asked.

"Nah, young and single in San Francisco. I'm sure he has better things to do."

Cross pulled back the covers on his bed, climbed in. With the remote, he clicked on the television.

In the dark room, staring back at the glaring eye of the television, he could easily have been home.

Shortly before midnight, Shanahan and Maureen crawled into bed. The lights were out, but the lights from the streets cast the room in light that could have come from the moon.

"What do we do tomorrow?"

"Rent a car, go up and see my grandson," Shanahan said. "What do you think?"

131

Eighteen

They picked up a car near Union Square and drove up Highway 101 across the Golden Gate Bridge, cutting over to Highway 1 near Mill Valley. Shanahan was nervous. He stuttered a bit on the phone earlier in the morning as he announced his presence in the Bay Area and his intention of visiting if that wouldn't conflict with the plans of his son, daughter-in-law, and grandson.

They were happy about it. It was summer. The whole family was working in the vineyard, but that didn't preclude a visit and a special dinner that afternoon.

"Come on up," his son, Ty, said enthusiastically.

They had invited Cross, but he declined, saying he wanted to check on Channing, find out if he was staying on or leaving town, though there wasn't much anyone could do no matter what decision the guy made.

The highway wound around hills and overlooked the sunny, rocky coast. The only drive with more curves was the road to Hana in Maui, so the going was slower than Shanahan had imagined and they arrived later than they anticipated. It made no difference to the California Shanahans.

Ty was in his mid forties, slender like his father, dark-haired as his father once was, but more cheerful. Ty's wife was strikingly beautiful. An Asian woman, she possessed a quiet, but happy charm, that she passed on to their son. Jason was a young man with eyes that suggested mischief as well as cheer.

Jason gave his grandfather and step-grandmother—the latter a title that was never spoken of—a tour of the winery, while his parents caught up with what had to be done that day.

Shanahan's grandson had visited Indianapolis once and seemed to enjoy the experience. He was fascinated with Shanahan's late career choice and got along well with Maureen. Now it was his turn to play host, not at all bored with his assignment.

In the city, the cold, gray morning fog was gone by noon. Earlier, Cross took two cups of coffee and a bagel in a coffee shop on Sutter, watching as the local suits, newspapers fluttering, mixed with the tourists, maps unfolding. Many of the visitors wore short-sleeve shirts and shorts and no doubt cursed San Francisco's failure to deliver California's promise of sunny warmth.

Cross walked up Bush to the Grant Hotel. He checked with the desk clerk, a young Asian man in a Nike hat, to see if Lester Channing was still registered. He was. Was he registered for tomorrow? he asked him.

"Did you want to see Mr. Channing?" he asked, apparently suspecting Cross's inquiry might not be so innocent.

"No, I wanted to drop something by tomorrow afternoon," Cross said, quickly manufacturing a story, "and I wanted it to be a surprise. But I'm not sure when he's leaving."

"Actually," he said, "he's checking out at two."

"Oh goodness," Cross said, "I guess I need to get busy." He almost laughed. He suddenly felt like Aunt Bee on the Andy Griffith show.

Cross left, picked up a newspaper and another cup of coffee and staked out a place across the street. If Channing was looking around, he'd see Cross pretty easily, more easily than picking up Cross's tail earlier in the investigation. Cross didn't mind. He hoped that would be the case.

He waited slightly less than an hour before he saw Channing leave the hotel. He carried a satchel and walked west. He hadn't seen Cross. In less than a block, Channing entered A Summer Place.

A Summer Place, Cross found out as he entered from the strong sun into the dim bar, wasn't particularly summery, save the six-foot-tall advertisement for Corona beer, featuring a man in a sombrero. Cross didn't think the Mexicans would like it. At any rate there wasn't much there there. Half a dozen tables, jukebox, and a big man at the bar with a draft beer.

It was clear to Cross that Channing was on his way home. He checked out of the hotel but it was still too early for the airport. And why pay the tab at an airport bar when it was cheaper to sip in a neighborhood bar? And this was a neighborhood bar. Nothing here for the tourists. Plainer than Harry's. Only those things a bar needs. No froufrou.

Cross sat at the next stool.

"Howdy partner," he said cheerfully.

"Got nothing for you," Channing said.

"No, you already gave." Cross motioned for the bartender to bring them both a beer. "Just wanted to thank you for paying your bill."

Channing gave him a look.

"I see you talked with your wife," Cross added.

"I'm not done with you," Channing said.

"Looks like the dance is going to continue then," Cross said. "Anyway, here." Cross handed Channing his wallet. "You dropped that the other night at the Boom Boom Room."

Channing glared. He was smart enough not to do anything that would land him in the county jail. Cross knew that too.

"The pieces are all falling into place," Cross continued. "You might want to make your peace with the IPD when you get back. It'll go easier if you cooperate. I don't have to tell you that, right?"

Channing said nothing.

"Too late to cover tracks," Cross said. The four cups of coffee and glass of beer kicked in.

"Listen," Cross said conspiratorially, "I'm going to take a little trip to the john and if you're not here when I get back, don't worry your pretty little head about it. I know where to find you."

Channing said nothing, stared ahead as if there were something worth watching amidst the bottled shelves on the back bar. As Cross walked back to the restroom, he wondered if he put Channing's nose on a chalk line would he be paralyzed. It worked for chickens, they said.

A few seconds later, Channing came into the bathroom. Cross was at the urinal and didn't see him until the guy was right up on him. Cross felt a quick, hard punch to the kidney. Involuntarily Cross arched backward before dropping to his knees.

"I'm a sentimental guy," Channing said. "I didn't want to leave without saying goodbye."

Channing nodded before he turned to leave.

Cross wanted to say something, but the only thought in his pain-ridden brain was "Your mother wears combat boots," so he decided to stay quiet. He got slowly to his feet. The pain began to subside a bit, but he'd carry both bruises with him for days—the one on his kidney and the one for his ego. Cross sat at the bar.

"Another?" the bartender asked.

"My kidneys couldn't stand it," Cross said.

"The big guy said you were picking up the tab."

"He'll pay in the end," Cross said with more bitterness than he intended to convey. The bartender gave him a suspicious look, then a smile, picked up the ten Cross had tossed his way.

"A man on a mission," the man said.

Cross pondered that thought a few moments. He wondered what his mission was. The smaller mission was to get Channing in jail and get a little justice for a dead woman. But was there something else he was doing or should be doing with his life? Well, he told himself, he never quite knew that. At 40, it didn't seem likely that he ever would. The next question was obvious. Did he care?

The sweet corn reminded Shanahan of summers with his dad and mom in Wisconsin. However, the zucchini, the portabella mushrooms, and grilled halibut were not usually part of his Midwest upbringing. They served something called "heir-loom" tomatoes, which were exactly like the flavor-filled tomatoes he knew as a youth.

The air was sweet. The sky here seemed bigger, the sun more golden.

"You have a nice life, Ty," Shanahan said.

"I do," he said. "And today you guys made it nicer." He sipped his glass of chilled Chardonnay as the elder Shanahan had moved from his clear bottle of Miller High Life beer to his own glass of clear Chardonnay.

"You need to come out sometime and spend a few weeks," Ty's wife, Qin Qin, said.

"I hope you do," Jason said.

Shanahan wondered what he had done to deserve such fine treatment. Ty's life was just fine thanks in no part to Shanahan's role as a father. He hadn't deserted his son those many years ago. His late wife took the ten-year-old away. But Shanahan had made no attempt to find either one of them, content at the time to seethe in quiet anger, or wallow in self-pity or put the whole affair in a mental box and keep it out of his sight.

There was enough to feel worry about if he felt so inclined. As Shanahan gathered the golden sunlight, his mind went back to young Todd. He was hounded by the law for a crime he might not have done. On the other hand, no one had yet proved who hired Channing. And Nina Moore, or whoever the hell she was, wasn't a whole lot safer than before. Certainly, she was unwilling to shed any further light on the situation. Had this little trip west accomplished anything at all except validate their previously held theories?

The setting didn't allow for self-centered introspection or castigation. The younger Shanahans had invited some friends over to share dinner. Apparently Ty had not inherited the father's reclusive nature or his reluctance to laugh and have a good time.

Ty was friendly and open, his wife was beautiful and gracious, and their son was warm and smiling.

They sat outside at a long table, with fresh vegetables, chilled bottles of wine, light conversation. The sun warmed the flesh while the breeze cooled it.

The crowd dispersed after dinner. Some went for walks.

Shanahan sank into a chaise lounge and looked out at the landscape, the grapevines climbing over the rolling hills in the foreground, smooth, round green hills in the distance. Thoughts of murder, war, famine, dissipated in the atmosphere of an almost too perfect paradise. The mind was further cajoled into heavenly contentment by fine food and the introduction of the fermented grape to gently and wonderfully modify the pulse going through the synapses of his brain. Shanahan's mind was somewhere, drifting, pleasantly confusing his son Ty with his own younger self, thinking for a strange and enchanted moment that he was back in Wisconsin. He drifted awhile, half asleep, half awake until the sun began to edge near the horizon.

"I'm afraid we have to get back," Shanahan said to no one. He looked around. They were all gathered at the long, raised fishpond beside the walkway that led to the building where the wooden barrels sat in controlled coolness.

"I'm afraid we have to go," Shanahan said again, this time with an audience. "Early plane tomorrow."

Ty walked his father and Maureen to the car.

"You've done well out here," Shanahan said. "All on your own."

"Not completely," he said. "I have Qin Qin. She's my inspiration."

"Hard to imagine you owning a winery. You know," Shanahan said, "if we had all gone back to Wisconsin, I guess you would have started a brewery."

Ty laughed. "Who knows? Life worked out. It is good and I'm as happy as it is possible to be and still be sane."

"Good family," Shanahan said. He didn't know exactly what to say, which was good, because he would have no idea how to say it. All he knew was that he was glad Ty turned out the way he did, though it was both a burden lifted and an indictment. His contribution wasn't necessary after all.

The goodbyes were warm and heartfelt. The drive back was bittersweet. When the escape ends, Shanahan thought, we are

137

left with the world as it is. On the other hand, perhaps there were ways to make it better—personally and in general. He thought about Pedersen and the Pedersen types. Yes, he did have more information than before. He knew Channing was involved and Channing was the road to discovery. More important, he knew Lianna never made the trip.

"What are you thinking?" Shanahan asked, as his rental car cleared the on ramp and moved into the middle lane.

Maureen looked surprised. "You never ask me that." She grinned. "You're a bit mellow, huh?"

"Nice afternoon."

"I'm thinking we could move to out here," she said. "I don't mean move in with your son or even nearby, just here. It gets awfully cold in Indianapolis in March, you know? You could relax, really retire."

"My golden years, is that what you're saying?"

"Why not?"

"You suppose the Hearst Castle is for sale?"

"Hey, anything is possible. Just some things more than others."

Cross moved from bar to bar, thinking the hotel room was a far too claustrophobic place to spend an afternoon. He had to hit his emergency credit card. Just as Bart Maverick clipped a $500 bill inside the lapel of his jacket, Cross kept a virgin credit card with a $2500 limit. And now he was in a profound what-the-hell mood.

He picked up a late lunch on Belden Alley, where a string of European restaurants spilled out into a carless street. It was all very continental, he thought, surprised that he liked it, surprised that it had the ability to lighten his mood. The service was appropriately slow, condoning laziness, aimlessness. It was his kind of place in the same way Nina Moore was his kind of singer.

Knowing that Shanahan wouldn't be back until evening, Cross lingered in a bookstore, roaming the aisles—travel, photography, music. Only his bruised and aching kidneys reminded him why he was in San Francisco.

He was tired enough to nap and headed back to the hotel. Looking up the street that climbed the hill, he could see the fog descending, quickly like a tidal wave. He could feel the cold and wet.

"Little cats' feet, my ass," Cross said to no one in particular.

Nineteen

C ross was up early enough. His suitcase was packed and he was waiting in the lobby of the hotel.

"I'm not going," Cross said, suddenly.

"What do you mean?" Maureen asked. "You're booked."

"I can't leave her here," he said.

"What do you intend to do? Kidnap her?" Shanahan asked. "We need the law, I'm afraid. And what makes you think you can find her? She could change her name again and head for Jamaica. How do you even intend to go about this?"

"I don't know."

"You said that Channing checked out. He's not going to kill her now."

"He checked out of the hotel. Did he check out of the city?" Cross asked. "Who knows what Channing's up to. Anyway, I'll find her. A bird's gotta sing. At least this one does. And in more ways than one."

"Where are you going to be? Here?" Maureen asked.

"I'm going to try to get into Channing's hotel. It's cheaper."

"Pretty nice of you," Maureen said, kissing him on the cheek.

"No, not deserving of praise," Cross said. He wasn't and he knew it. There was no doubt he'd like to close the case on Channing and it would take more information from the dancer turned singer. He also didn't want to go back. He would find Margot there. He would have to deal with her. He would have to deal with his feelings. He wouldn't have a choice. He wouldn't tell Shanahan and Maureen though. He told no one.

* * *

140

Cross checked into the Grant. He wondered if it were named after Ulysses, Cary or Hugh. The young man behind the desk was gone. In his place was a pleasant, pretty much all-business Asian woman. She gave the young detective confidence that he hadn't checked into a fleabag hotel. The lobby was unpretentious yet clean, qualities he found in his room as well.

Settled, he went out into the world in search of coffee, perhaps breakfast. He could feel hunger moving from his brain, inching its way to his belly as he walked. He passed by a marquee that boasted the best naked male dancers inside. Probably still too early for naked dancers of any gender, he thought. He pulled the *San Francisco Chronicle* from the news box.

There were deaths and celebrities and celebrities mixed up in death. The city was fighting a scandal. He was now down to the gates of Chinatown on Bush. He tried to imagine a Chinese breakfast and decided against the adventure. He turned the other direction, heading into the shopping district. Someone somewhere had to serve eggs and potatoes to the morning rush hour.

The morning was overcast but not foggy. Cool, but not biting cold. He walked. Retail stores weren't open yet. But there was traffic and lots of folks walking purposefully, presumably to work. He found himself in the high-rent district—Armani, Burberry, Saks Fifth Avenue, Neiman Marcus and many names he didn't recognize but whose store windows suggested he couldn't even put a down payment on a T-shirt. No diners.

The judgement about whether it was more likely a little greasy spoon was this way or that way fought for time in his brain as it battled the nagging question about his purpose for staying on. He had to find a legitimate reason to stay so he wouldn't feel like so much of a coward.

The city seemed smaller than it was when they left as they headed into it on the freeway. Shanahan's ancient Chevy

Malibu cut through the city to get to Michigan Street, where it had a clear shot to the Eastside. He had never realized how few people walk on the streets here. Indianapolis was a very different city than San Francisco. The streets were wider. There was more space between homes, between people, perhaps between people's lives.

It was home. He felt the tension slip from his old bones.

"The day is almost gone," Maureen said, adjusting her watch.

They left in the morning. It was now late afternoon.

Shanahan was eager to share his information with Kowalski, maybe with Lt. Swann. He could prove nothing yet, but he could point both of them in a better direction, give some ammunition to Evans's defense attorney, give credence to Swann's suspicions. Though Shanahan didn't have a direct link between Channing and Pedersen, he now knew who to try to connect. And he had a better picture of Pedersen—a far different one than the public had.

Harry was just leaving as Shanahan and Maureen pulled into the driveway.

"Exercised, fed, watered and peed," Harry said, referring to the animals that had been left in his charge.

"You didn't get Einstein to exercise, Harry."

"True. You don't get Einstein to do anything he doesn't want to do. He's a lot like you." Harry looked at Maureen, winked. "He even looks a lot like you. All bony and creaky."

"That really hurts coming from a Tom Cruise kind of guy like you."

"And crotchety."

Inside, Shanahan found Kowalski's number and called him.

"I need a little bit of your time," Shanahan said.

"I'm ready to leave. Come out to my place. Evans is there."

"He's out?"

"Didn't want to stay at his place, so I'm putting him up for awhile."

"Good, I need to talk to both of you."

"Give me a headline on this?" Kowalski asked.

"We found the girl who rode on Lianna's ticket."

"I see," Kowalski said somberly. "Any more on her?"

"She's not cooperative. But she's connected to an ex-cop, current security firm owner by the name of Lester Channing. Not a very nice guy. You might want to run that by your client, Mr. Kowalski. I hope he doesn't know him."

"I'll be home in an hour. You know Ravenswood?"

"You've got Todd Evans in Ravenswood?" Shanahan asked, surprised. It was a strange, reclusive, remote, xenophobic, all white river community along the seemingly appropriately named White River in the city. It was hard to find, a fact the inhabitants liked. Certainly no one went to Ravenswood on the way to some place else. Seemed perfect for a biker rebel like Kowalski, but he wasn't so sure about the reception Evans would get.

"C'mon, its nearly civilized," Kowalski said, laughing. "You afraid?"

"No. I know Ravenswood. Me, my car, and my old hound dog, we fit in."

"Bring the dog," Kowalski said. "They're my favorite people."

At eleven, Cross was back in his apartment. He put a call in to Nick Lang.

"Thought you were gone," Nick said.

"Bad penny."

"Where are you?"

"I checked into Channing's old hotel. Forty a night and cable TV."

"I'd invite you to stay with me," Nick said, "but I'm living in my office. I shower at the gym."

"That's not why I called."

"Let's get together, have a bite to eat. I know where Nina Moore is tonight if you're still interested."

"How do you know that?"

"Some guys I know, they're following her."

"Following her?"

"I don't mean tailing, I mean following her career. She's a sensation, they tell me. There's a place on Valencia. Kind of open mike kind of thing, except most everybody is pretty good. Not karaoke. Good backup group. I've been there a couple of times. Why don't you come down to my office around six? We'll walk over to the Mission, grab a bite to eat and catch her act."

"This is great."

Ravenswood had changed some since Shanahan last visited. No cars up on concrete blocks or "no trespassing" signs visible from the road. But there was a certain quality about the houses and yards that suggested the residents weren't buying into the American Dream. One wouldn't expect these folks to spend a lot of time perusing a Williams-Sonoma catalog or settling back with a cup of tea to watch *Antiques Roadshow*. Then again, Shanahan thought, he wasn't entirely out of place here either.

Kowalski's white frame house with its back to the river was in pretty good shape. No broken windows. The paint wasn't peeling. The yard was mowed, though it wasn't likely anyone would describe the flora and fauna as manicured. Sunflowers, eight foot tall, looked wild and out of control. A huge weeping willow bowed over the river.

Kowalski came out, in jeans but with his white shirt still on, to greet Shanahan and Casey. Casey, who rarely took to men right away, had no problem with the bearded wild man.

"Come in, come in," he said. "Let me get you guys a beer."

"Casey doesn't drink," Shanahan said, stepping inside.

"I hope it's not a religious thing, because I plan to have one."

With a great deal of effort, a big, bow-legged bulldog came to its feet and slowly made his way to Casey. After a couple of sniffs, the bulldog went back to his spot on the wood floor and clunked down. Casey seemed equally uninterested, settling his bones down on the floor by the door. Casey, like Shanahan, wanted to know the way out before he went in.

"Two old guys," Kowalski said, "you'd think they'd have something to talk about."

Todd Evans came in from what looked to be the kitchen. He smiled with warmth but without conviction. The living room was huge, open to the roof. All wood. There were two big leather chairs and a massive gray corduroy-covered sofa. The art on the wall looked Mexican or South American, much more colorful than the furniture and walls. On one wall was a bookshelf, floor to where a ceiling might be in an average home. Art books, literature. Nothing that looked legal.

"So what did you expect?" Kowalski asked with humor.

"I thought your décor would feature more chains," Shanahan said. "Maybe some leather and spikes."

"And naked women?"

Shanahan nodded.

"You've got some information for us?" Kowalski asked.

"And some questions," Shanahan said. He looked at Todd, who was nearly swallowed by the sofa. "You up to it?"

"Definitely," he said, taking a deep breath.

"Child isn't yours, is it?" Shanahan asked.

"No," Todd said.

"Whose?"

"Don't know."

"But you knew all along because you had a vasectomy."

"Yes."

"Why didn't you tell anyone about this?"

Todd took a long time to answer. "I'm not sure there was one reason. I guess I hoped that it wasn't true, that maybe the doctor didn't do the procedure right, or that if we didn't talk about it, it wouldn't seem true. I'm not making any sense, I know. It doesn't make sense to me either."

"Who is the father?" Kowalski asked, bringing Shanahan a bottle of beer.

"I don't know."

"You suspect someone?" Shanahan asked.

"Her boss. As far as I know that's the only person she spent a lot of time with. She was real taken with him. Some kind of hero. I mean she loves me, I know. But she used to look at me as if I were really, really special. After spending time with him . . . he was older, wealthier, more sophisticated, more powerful, and very, very smart in the way she thought she was smart . . . I was just another kid on the block."

"Your relationship was over, wasn't it?" Kowalski asked.

"Yep." Evans looked as if he was on the verge of tears.

"That's what the fight was about. She was, in fact, leaving you. For good," Kowalski continued.

"She was going to come back for her things."

"You said she looked at her watch just before she left?"

"Yes."

"She had to be somewhere," Shanahan said to Kowalski.

"You didn't know where she was going?" Kowalski asked Evans.

"No. I assumed it would be Mary Beth. They were pretty close, especially in the last few months. They talked about maternity things; you know, hormone levels, morning sickness. Mary Beth is a physician, so I think Lianna relied on her more than before."

"Schmidt?" Shanahan asked surprised. "Mary Beth Schmidt is a doctor? I thought she was the head of operations?"

"As I understand it, many of the company's top executives are doctors. Doctors and chemists or both."

"Listen, Todd," Shanahan said, sitting on the sofa a few feet away from Evans. "Wherever Lianna is, she isn't in San Francisco. We found what amounts to Lianna's double. She made the trip."

Todd Evans was quiet, perhaps trying to understand all of the implications.

"Where is she?" he asked, though he had to know there wasn't an answer to that one in the room.

"Todd, do you know a guy named Lester Channing?" Shanahan asked.

There wasn't a flicker of recognition or shock or anything in Evans's eyes, save bewilderment.

"No. Don't think so. Who is he?"

"He is connected in some way to Lianna's look-alike. Now what we need to know is who he's connected to at the other end."

Kowalski checked his watch, walked over to Evans and then past him and on to the large television set that dominated one wall, speaking as he went. "This is important. You're sure you don't know him?" He picked up the remote and clicked it on.

"No," Todd Evans said.

The sound from the TV set startled the young man. Heads turned. A huge hamburger occupied the screen before the familiar tune introduced the network news.

Twenty

Nick Lang was waiting when Cross came out of the Grant Hotel. He'd parked his old Alfa Romeo sedan in the white zone.

"You're early," Cross said, getting in.

"You never know when there will be a parade or electrical failure," Nick said. "After rush hour. Things slow a bit."

Night had nearly fallen, but the fog had relented. Nick's little car spirited down through the shopping area, across Market, and turned right.

"I really appreciate your help," Cross said. "This is beyond the call."

"I don't get out much. This is good. Maybe it will remind me why I moved here." He grinned a half grin. "Plus I enjoy showing tourists around. So that means dinner is on you."

It was a Vietnamese restaurant on Valencia and 16th, very plain; so hopefully inexpensive. Cross went to the john, and when he came back Nick was on the phone and didn't see Cross approach. Cross had a moment to see what that bartendress at the strip joint saw earlier—the two of them were same model, same year of white guy. Both of them had the physique of the slightly gone-to-seed lifeguard. Nick's hair and complexion were lighter, and in Cross's mind, they both came up a nickel short of being good looking. Nick wore jeans and a light sport jacket over a T-shirt. That was Cross's uniform as well. The only difference was that Nick wore running shoes, something that a former cop would never wear except when he was running.

Nick said something quickly and quietly and folded up his phone.

148

"She's really on tonight?" Cross said, shaking his head in disbelief. He sat down, and looked at the menu. He didn't recognize anything, but the price seemed right. "Yep. Not sure when. So we might have to spend some time listening to jazz." "I could think of worse things," Cross said. "But I am amazed you already know where she went." "Small town, like I said. And though I don't know a whole lot of folks, I know someone who loves jazz and follows it religiously. He . . . well, this person especially likes to pick the rising stars. Your Nina Moore is one of them."

The older anchorman spoke authoritatively. "Missing still in Indianapolis is Noah Rose and Company's executive Lianna Bailey. The police have released her boyfriend, Todd Evans, on bond. Not everyone is happy about that fact. The police are not telling anyone where he's gone. The city's Citizens Concerned for Victims' Justice, has suggested that not knowing the alleged Evans's whereabouts means there is a murderer in their midst."

"You scared, Shanahan?" Kowalski asked, flicking off the TV.

"This is the midst right here," Shanahan said.

Evans tried to smile.

"Here's the thing," Kowalski said. "What they're really saying is we don't have any news at all today and we really don't have any news about Lianna Bailey, but she is what we're talking about today, so we have to find a new way to say Lianna Bailey is still missing."

"What did you expect? Journalism?"

"Tell me if I'm wrong," Kowalski said. "You're old enough to remember. There was a time when the news didn't have commercials. Right?"

Shanahan nodded. "As I understood it, because these networks and TV stations had free use of the airwaves, they had to provide so many hours of public service. News was part of that."

"Now, news is entertainment," Kowalski said. "All right, I'm off the soapbox for a moment or two. What do we do about the girl in San Francisco?"

"Cross is still out there. I don't know yet."

"If Lianna is still alive," Todd said, his voice dry and unsure. "If she's alive, she might be in danger. We don't have time."

Optimism might be a good thing, Shanahan thought, but in the end it can be crushing.

"I'm going to talk with Swann, let him know about Channing and the singer." Shanahan went to the door. Casey followed. "When is all of this going to court?" Shanahan asked.

Kowalski walked them out to the car and out of earshot.

"If Evans is guilty, the longer it goes, the worse it is. If he's innocent, I wish it were tomorrow. Let me know what the singer says." Kowalski knelt down and rubbed Casey behind the ears. "If you can't get her to come back, get her to make a sworn statement. If it goes to trial we're going to need her in person. So let's keep track of her. Don't want to try to get her back from Brazil."

"Look into the life and times of Lester Channing. He was a cop in Cincinnati once upon a time."

"Now there's a town." He shook his head. He didn't mean it nicely.

"Marge Schott isn't there anymore," Shanahan said.

"There's a few of her still around, I suspect." Kowalski got to his feet, turned to walk back in. "Come by anytime," Kowalski said.

"Thanks," Shanahan said.

"I was talking to Casey. If he brings you, well, that's fine too."

The two impoverished private investigators walked down Valencia a few blocks before cutting over to Mission Street.

It was hard to pin down the Valencia Street neighborhood— a mix of yuppie and bohemia with assorted other eccentric touches. Lots of bookstores, new and used. Coffee shops. He noticed an Indian ice-cream shop. Is curry really a flavor? Once they were on Mission, the Latin flavor took over full force. It was a neighborhood that was both alive and down on its luck. Cross recognized some drug deals going down, noticed the lowriders on the street. Bars, liquor stores. Big old movie houses on this wide street were shut down or transformed, but the marquees were still up. Little markets with lots of fresh produce lined the streets.

"The Mission has many streets. Mission Street is just the main one," Nick said. "Dolores Street is pretty upscale. Guerrero is a basic everyday neighborhood. Valencia is being gentrified. And Mission is the heart. Tough, loud, fun, and dangerous."

"We get to choose?"

"Usually," Nick said, as they entered Club Savanna near 26th Street.

Maureen sensed Shanahan's get-things-done mood as he came into the kitchen. He had taken no notice of Casey. He went to the phone immediately. It was only after he waited for someone to pick up the line on the other end that he noticed Maureen was in the midst of a very complicated dinner.

Open on the countertop was her new cookbook *Sonoma County and Napa Valley Cuisine*. She noticed him looking and dropped a dishtowel over the word, "cuisine."

She looked at him, smiled. "Forget that it says 'cuisine.'"

"Yes, I'm calling for Lieutenant Swann," Shanahan said into the phone. He showed his disappointment. "Can you have him call me?"

Shanahan looked at counter and table. "What's all this?" he asked.

"Food. Eventually good food."

"I don't recognize some of this. The ginger, yes. What's this?" Shanahan lifted up some green leaves.

"Basil. And you know garlic."

Shanahan noticed the sesame oil and the rice vinegar.

"Are we drinking this?"

"I'm not. You can if you want," she said, calling his bluff. "Actually, this is a perfect dinner for beer. I've taken the liberty of getting us some pale ale from the Sierras."

"Pale ale?" he grimaced. The ringing of the phone ambushed further comment.

"Shanahan," he said.

"You called."

"A guy named Channing helped a Lianna Bailey look-alike get on a plane for San Francisco."

"You know that?"

"I met her. Cross is in San Francisco now, trying to convince her to cooperate."

"Tell you what. For now, all we need is a notarized statement acknowledging what she did. Though it would be better, she doesn't have to come back right now to get things rolling. Also, if somebody gets to her, we have the testimony anyway." There was a moment of quiet, but Shanahan was sure Swann wasn't done. "This is good. You're sure there's no connection between Channing and the kid?"

"I don't know that. He said there wasn't, so let's just let the chips fall."

"You get three notarized documents. Provide one to Kowalski, one to Rafferty or the DA and keep one in a safe place. I wish I could jump in, but I can't right now. At least not officially. I'll do some discreet checking on Channing."

That was it. All business. Nervous business from Swann.

"Here, at least try it," Maureen said, handing Shanahan a glass of pale ale.

He took a sip, shrugged. It was good, but he didn't want to admit it too readily or he'd be trying all sorts of new things. Maureen had opened him up to many new experiences in the few years they'd known each other. His old reclusive self saw no reason to try anything new. Sticking with what he already knew meant warding off disappointment. But now—even in his golden years—he was changing. Old dogs. New tricks. What do you know?

Change had been easy and almost always for the better.

Shanahan had lived with his first wife's taste long after she left. When Maureen wanted to redo some things he didn't object. She couldn't do worse, he thought. He was pleasantly surprised. She didn't make everything pink and delicate. The flowered wallpaper that stubbornly stuck to the walls for thirty years was gone. In its place were painted walls in warm pastel grays and browns.

The things he liked, his desk and chair in the living room, remained untouched, though the carpet was replaced. Years of Einstein and Casey made it impossible to keep. There were more pots and pans in the kitchen than before and always a vase of fresh flowers on the hall table. He had come to like that brightness in his life as well as the light she brought him naturally. She didn't turn the house into a place where the ladies took tea, he thought as she prepared the food and he counted his blessings. It amused him for a moment to think of Maureen taking tea.

"I'll have to get you a chef's hat," he told her, watching how seriously she took her culinary work.

"I'll have to get you an orange wig, a big red nose and some size eighteen shoes," she said. "Why don't you go outside and play with Casey?"

"I will," he said. "But I have to make a call first. Let Cross know what he has to do."

She sang slow even when the notes were fast. The result was a kind of carefree sadness in her voice—life speeding by without her. Nina Moore made the song, each song, her own.

"I'm only happy when I'm sad," she said between songs, letting a little grin play on her lips.

The Savanna Club wasn't a whole lot different from the Boom Boom Room, except that they served food. There was a bar along one side, tables in the wider area and a stage in the corner. The art on the wall was record album jackets. Nice place. But Cross, with all his strip bar visits and now jazz club encounters, was beginning to feel like a lounge lizard.

They had waited through three singers before Nina Moore

153

showed up and sang a couple of songs—this time with a Latin edge. She was versatile, Cross thought. Singer, dancer, accomplice.

The band took a time out. At the table—Nick convinced her to join them—her first words were: "I don't want to go back there, and I'm not talking about a place. That's all a million miles away from me now."

"There's a woman. She looks a lot like you," Cross said. "She may be dead. She may be held captive somewhere."

"If that's the truth, I don't know, but I didn't have anything to do with any of that. Mine was a straight deal. Here's the ticket, here's some money—"

"There was also the charge card. And there's the ring," Cross said, nodding toward the yellowish diamond on her hand that Shanahan mentioned earlier. "That was hers too."

". . . and start a new life. That's what I've done."

"I'm sorry," Cross said, "but you haven't escaped. They can come and get you anytime. They can find you anywhere, arrest you, and try you for kidnapping, a federal offense, or murder if that's what it turns out to be."

"I didn't—" she started to protest.

"It doesn't matter. You helped him commit a crime. You participated. You were part of the plan. What did you think when he told you to use her card? What did you think when he told you to use her cell phone to call her boyfriend?"

It was as if she finally got it, understood the situation. That didn't mean she liked it. And it didn't mean she liked Cross. She glared at him.

"He's not the bad guy," Nick said. "Your friend who gave you that deal that was too good to be true is the bad guy."

"For now tell us what you know, get it on record," Cross said.

"Funny thing is you already know everything I know. Mr. Channing saw me at the club and we . . . uh . . . talked, and a few weeks later he came in and proposed this deal."

"When you talked," Cross said, "you told him about your dream of a new life?"

"Yeah, I did. I did just that." She shook her head and looked as if she were about to cry.

Cross didn't ask her if she was happy now.

"How much money?" Cross asked.

"Not your business," she said sharply.

"It will come out," Cross said. "It will help us trace the money back to its origins."

"Thirty thousand."

"You didn't suspect anything?" Cross asked.

"Wasn't my business," she said. She caught herself. "I didn't want to know."

"Why did you call Evans?"

"Who?"

"Todd Evans."

"I don't know him," she said.

"You called someone when you arrived here. Why?"

"Just doing what I was told. Call. Hang up when someone answers. Then toss the phone. I didn't know who I was calling or why."

When your dreams come true, are you supposed to question it? Wasn't there something about looking a gift horse in the mouth? Cross thought. He felt sorry for her. Of course he felt sorry for Margot and for himself. He didn't feel sorry for Channing. If Cross had made it even, the kidney punch put Channing ahead. What? Was this a game with winners and losers? You bet. Cross nodded his head.

"What?" Nick asked.

"Oh nothing," Cross said.

"We're going to need you to sign some papers tomorrow," Cross told Nina Moore.

She looked wary. How was he going to make sure she was around for the notary public?

"I can be on your side when the case comes up. Or not."

155

Twenty-One

Howie Cross was dead on his feet. He drank coffee non-stop and tried to stop himself from blinking, fearful that he would drift off to sleep and miss his flight. He'd squeezed on an American Trans Air flight with a minimum of penalty, though he would gladly have mortgaged his soul, though he wasn't sure he still had one, to get back to his little trans-formed chauffeur's quarters and sleep for three days.

In his jacket were the three copies of Nina's or Norah's or whoever in the hell she was's statement. Each was notarized. To get it he had to stake out her place all night for fear she'd sneak out and head to Biloxi or Buenos Aires. But he got it. He was almost too tired to gloat. Almost. He was thrilled to have the piece of paper that would destroy Channing and, he quickly added to his mental inventory of good deeds, help discover the whereabouts of one Lianna Bailey.

He had also had a chance to talk with the singer as they taxied to an office near Japantown to get the statements nota-rized. She was someone who was determined to get ahead, someone who did what she had to do to get where she wanted to go. She knew what she wanted to do when she was five years old, she told him.

"I still don't know what I want to do when I grow up," Cross said.

"You'll be fine," she said. "I can see these things. And I can see it in you."

He gave her his card, said to let him know when her first CD came out.

It seemed as if only a moment had passed from the time

he'd ensconced himself in seat 20A and being awakened by an attendant, announcing his arrival at Indianapolis International Airport. He wasn't as tired, but now he was just plain irritable. His neck ached, he felt drained of all energy, and whatever feelings of satisfaction he may have had earlier melted into a kind of angry ennui.

Margot had spent some time there. There were cigarette butts stamped out in various plates around the living room, bedroom, kitchen and bath. Otherwise she had been fairly neat. There was half a bottle Absolut on the kitchen counter, some magazines in the bedroom, and a half-eaten box of chocolates on the bed stand. Then it got scary. He found three pairs of high heels on the floor near the chair and some expensive lingerie on the chair.

She would be coming back. He tried to remember what date it was. She'd be gone. The race was over. The next big race was August. He'd have June and July to change his name, undergo plastic surgery, and find a new home.

Among the many things Emile Morales provided Shanahan were the names of two people who left Mason Life Systems with Pedersen. One chose to leave. That was Mary Beth Schmidt. The other was Victor Louden, who was asked to leave, presumably, Morales had said, because of his perceived loyalty to the outgoing CEO. Morales assumed that Louden would be working with Pedersen. But according to the Noah Rose & Company website, Louden was not listed among the officers or senior staff though he had been quite senior at Mason Life Systems—executive vice president heading up Research & Development.

Did Louden find another job? Did he retire?

Sometimes, Shanahan thought, you can tell right away. What the detective saw in the small studio apartment at Ninth and Pennsylvania was a broken man. Tall, slouching, with wispy reddish hair over a balding scalp, Louden had a way of looking up at Shanahan even when he stood taller. His pale-blue eyes were lifeless and he spoke as if every sentence was an apology.

157

"He promised," Louden said. "Otherwise I wouldn't have moved here. I burned bridges for him. I'm not sure who would have me."

Early on he had some possibilities in New Jersey and Massachusetts and even in Austin, Texas. But Louden was convinced that Mason Life Systems wouldn't recommend him and that apparently Pedersen wouldn't either. Pedersen wasn't returning Louden's calls.

"Why didn't you go knock on his door, or pay him an office visit?"

"Oh," Louden said, shaking his head as if he'd just seen the grim reaper. "One does not confront Mr. Pedersen."

"Mister? I thought you guys were close."

Louden's laugh was haunting.

The only reason Louden agreed to talk with Shanahan was the mention of Emile Morales. Morales didn't hate him, Louden said. Perhaps Morales could help him get his career back on track. Shanahan didn't encourage the thought. What Shanahan remembered was Morales feeling sorry for Louden, saying that he was a brilliant man who fell into the Pedersen cult—in a way that suggests one doesn't return from that particular abyss.

Shanahan sat on a stack of boxes near the window.

"Mr. Louden, how difficult is it to clone something?"

Victor thought a moment. "It's not as hard as most people think; but you need something beyond Chem Lab 101."

"A human?"

"More complex than a kitten," Victor said, "but basically the same. You get a tissue biopsy. Maybe a skin cell. You do a culture of the sample and you remove the 'adult characteristics,' essentially regressing them back to a prebirth status. Next you get an egg, remove all the genetic material and inject the donor cell into the egg. Then it gets a little harder. You must work with it to produce a single-celled cloned embryo. When you do, you plant that in a host mother. After that, if things were done correctly, the rest is just a regular pregnancy."

"So it's possible to clone a human today?"

"Oh yes."

"Could Pedersen do it?"

"No, that's not his training. His background is in gene injection."

"What's that?" Shanahan asked, weary of the twenty-first century.

"Depending on how you look at it, it is the process of engineering traits in living beings. That's why Mr. Pedersen is such a big hit with Rose. They see pharmaceuticals in a far larger way than treatment of disease, but as a way of creating a more desirable you." He said the last few words with a hint of a smile.

"Taller?"

"Sure."

"More hair?"

"Yes, I'd have signed up for that," Louden said, loosening up. "Earlier thinking said that you could make designer babies. The thing is adults can reengineer themselves. You know how surgeons are making bundles of money using their skills to make someone look younger, or prettier. The surgeons better get the cash while they can. Because in a few years, there will be pills for that. People won't have to take a two-week vacation so the scars from their face-lift can heal. They will just take a pill daily and gradually they will look younger, or get stronger. I'm guessing the Olympics will be pretty amazing to watch in about twenty years. Beauty pageants." He seemed to drift off a bit. "It won't be fashion by Calvin Klein, it will be body by Calvin Klein. People will be designed."

"What do you know about Mary Beth Schmidt?"

"She's smarter, in a scientific sense, than he is. On the other hand, he lives in the real world." Louden had picked up some energy. A little life danced in his eyes.

"She doesn't."

"A smart, smart scientist, but a naive dreamer."

"Oh a question," Shanahan said as he headed for the door. "This injection thing. Can we make people live longer?"

159

"Absolutely," he said, having fully escaped from his shell, "but I'm afraid . . ." Then he stopped.

"What you're saying is for me not to get my hopes up?" Shanahan asked.

"Well you got to start sometime . . ."

"Before seventy, right?"

"Yep. Afraid so."

A dying breed, Shanahan thought.

Shanahan stopped by Harry's.

"Why do you look so pained, Deets?"

"Do I? It's just my face. That's the way it is."

"Well, you should do something about it. It's damned depressing." He slid under the bar and retrieved empties from one of the booths.

Shanahan went into the rest room, flicked on the light. He looked at himself. He did look a little weary, a little drawn, with brown bags under his eyes. He rubbed some cold water on his face. The trip, maybe. The visit with his son and his family had caused him some worry. It was nice and all that, Shanahan thought, but it still wasn't easy.

The other thing was that he had presumed that Lianna Bailey was dead. They usually are when someone like that comes up missing. Now he wasn't so sure. Maybe she was missing, and if that was the case, they should stop dawdling around. Time made a big difference, especially now that a couple of players were identified.

Shanahan drove over to Cross's place, found him home but not alone. Cross guided Shanahan into the living room, but in the kitchen, sitting in a cloud of smoke, was a beautiful woman. Dishwater blond they used to say about hair like that. Long neck. Elegant and sensual at the same time.

Shanahan felt he was cheating on Maureen for the thoughts that traveled the circuits of his brain. But they weren't gross thoughts, he told himself, merely an appreciation of nature's creativity.

Cross handed him the papers. "It's good," he said. "You want coffee?"

"You want me hanging around?" Shanahan asked.

"It's OK, really."

Shanahan sat down, looked through the one page notarized statement, signed by a Janet Jones.

"Are we sure that's her real name?" Shanahan asked as Cross came in with a cup of coffee, setting it on the small table near the older detective.

"As you read through it, you'll see that she accounts for all of her aliases. Pretty amazing. You know I hate the name Howard and especially Howie. So why don't I just change my name to something else?"

"Like what?"

"I don't know, something tougher. Rock, Stone, Brick . . ."

"Stump. I like Stump. Stumpy Cross."

"No, no. Something tough, that's just odd."

"How about Spanky? Spanky Cross. Kind of a baseball thing."

"If my hair were red, I could be Red Cross."

"People would give you money," Shanahan said.

"Yes, they would write me checks, but they would also expect me to be compassionate and help people. No, a tougher name. Cold, callous, mean."

"How about Lester as in Lester Channing?"

"All right, the game is over," Cross said.

"I think she's alive," Shanahan said. He was about to explain his thoughts when the slender woman appeared in the doorway. Shanahan stood politely.

"I'm Margot," she said. The light from the window to the side and behind her rendered her nightgown translucent and Shanahan caught the lines of her sleek body. She looked like a sexy angel.

"Shanahan," he said, fighting to avert his eyes, but not winning the battle convincingly. "I have places to go and people to see. Thanks," he said to Cross, holding up the papers. "This will get things moving a whole lot faster. For good or bad."

161

She moved to the side as Shanahan passed through the door. "Nice to see . . . meet you, Margot."

Outside, he took a deep breath. You'd think, he told himself, that it's well more than enough to have one beautiful woman on your mind. He reminded himself that the mind is not always practical or obedient. And he told himself that Maureen would find the incident cute. He would not tell Maureen.

Shanahan drove back toward Kowalski's office, feeling a bit like a Ping-Pong ball crisscrossing the city this way—a kind of giddy, silly Ping-Pong ball. Margot's scent, whatever it was, lingered as did her image.

Maybe the gene injection could turn back time. Funny, he thought, this from a man who for awhile actually looked forward to death. Now was a fine time for him to start enjoying life.

Twenty-Two

Kowalski was grinning when Shanahan came in. No one was with him. He wasn't on the phone.

"You've been telling yourself funny stories or do you need to be burped?"

"I enjoy my company, if that's what you mean. But you are right. I've got a story. We're going after Pedersen," Kowalski said, picking up a copy of the statement Shanahan had tossed on the desk. "The good news is that the D.A. is not only going to let us interview Pedersen, he is going to ask Pedersen to take a polygraph."

"I'll believe it when I see it," Shanahan said.

"You ready for the bad news? Channing's gone. His wife is distraught. He never came back from San Francisco or if he did he didn't return to their little bungalow. No one at his work admits knowing his whereabouts. In fact, they act like they don't know what to do. Channing signs the checks and it's not too long until payday."

"How did you find all this out?" Shanahan said.

"I picked up this little device," Kowalski said, lifting the phone from the receiver, "and the damnedest thing happened. I talked to people. I'm a smart guy."

"I'll just add Channing's house to my milk run," Shanahan said.

"One other thing," Kowalski said, standing, pulling a cigar from its cellophane wrapper. "Your restraining order has been lifted and we meet with the D.A. and Pedersen at nine in the morning. Be there."

"You're worth the money we're paying you," Shanahan said.

Kowalski laughed. "You sure know how to insult a guy."

"Thanks," Shanahan said.

"For what? Lifting the restraining order or commending you on your ability to insult?"

"You're a smart guy. You figure it out."

Shanahan swung by the Channings'. The van was in the drive- way. Nothing to lose, the old detective went to the door. The main door was open, he could see through the screen door as she approached.

She answered. Her eyes were dry, but red. She looked as if she hadn't slept in a week. This wasn't acting.

"What do you want?" she asked in such flat tones, Shanahan couldn't tell if she were angry, sad, or more likely the case, just didn't tell.

"You have any idea where he went?"

She shook her head "no."

"He has family living somewhere?"

She nodded.

"Where?"

"I don't know if I should be talking with you."

"I'll find out," Shanahan said. "And if the police—"

"They've been by. He has family in Cincinnati."

"Have you talked with them?"

"No." Flat emotionless speech.

"They haven't called you?"

"Why would they?"

"Friends? He has some guys he hangs out with?"

She shook her head. "They don't last long," she said. Shanahan thought he could detect some emotion there. Bitterness, he guessed.

"You OK?" Shanahan found himself asking, though a signif- icant part of his nature didn't want to know, especially if she wasn't.

"I'll get by," she said.

"Mrs. Channing. There's a missing woman. Somehow that's connected to your husband. Her life, if she's alive, is likely in jeopardy. Anything you can tell us about where Channing might be, or anything else about his behavior, anything you know . . ."

"I don't know anything," she said. "He didn't talk to me. He hasn't talked to me about anything for a long time." She had been beaten—at least emotionally—into admitting the unpleasant truth.

"That's why you hired Mr. Cross. You thought he was having an affair?"

"That's the pattern. I don't know why I bothered. Please let me go now. I'm very tired."

Shanahan felt a little tired too. He wished that after all these years he had learned to nap. Didn't all old people nap? They also played golf, joined AARP, saved coupons, and bought a condo in Florida. For Shanahan, it was 0 for 4. So much for stereotypes. He stopped by the O'Malia's food store downtown, picked up some halibut and lemons. His turn to cook.

"So," Maureen said, meeting him at the door and giving him a peck on the cheek. "What do you think of adding the Amalfi Coast?"

"To the drink menu?" he asked, moving toward the kitchen to set the groceries down. He knew better.

"If we go for a month, we can spend a few days in Venice, a week in Florence and Rome, maybe a few days in Sienna, and the rest on the beach."

A month. Shanahan had never thought about being away from home for that long since he left the Army.

"Halibut," Shanahan said. "Outside on the grill? Inside in the oven or pan fried?"

"The grill," she said. "I'll make the salad."

Here he was, Shanahan thought, living a normal life and Lianna Bailey, perhaps still alive, quite likely not living a normal life. Was she strapped to a chair in a warehouse, or was her disappearance willing? He had thoughts about why that might be the case as well. He should be doing something.

"Shanahan?" Maureen called to him. He looked at her.

"You're doing as much as you can as fast as you can."

He hoped that was the case. He looked forward to the Pedersen interview.

It was nine in the evening when Cross got the call from Shanahan telling him that Channing was missing and that the former cop had family in Cincinnati. That fit what Channing himself had told him. Maybe he could talk with Channing's parents. If that didn't work out—some parents forgive or over-look their children's assholiness—perhaps he could check out some Ohio property records on the computer. Maybe he would go over. A two-hour drive.

An internet search consumed a couple of the late-night hours, but eye-fatigue and the boring nature of going through bureaucratic websites, was enough to do him in. Done with an attempt at productive work, he faced the quiet hours before sleep with the now familiar and singularly depressing ques-tion—Margot. Was she going to show up tonight? It almost didn't matter. If she came he'd be disturbed. If she didn't, he would be disturbed. And in any event he'd have to wait to find out. She had the deck of cards in this sad, silly, little game.

Cross didn't check the time when he felt her body slide next to his. She smelled of whiskey and cigarettes.

Margot hadn't awakened him. He was lying on his back, staring up into the darkness, telling himself, lecturing himself at great length, on the need to let moments, hours, days unfold as they would. He told himself that he didn't need to stop his own momentum to wait for someone else to establish an agenda, that he, when opportunities—Margot included—presented themselves, he could welcome them or not, partic-ipate in, or extract himself from the situation. This was the way to live. Refuse to anticipate. Live in the moment. He had found several ways of telling himself all of this, staying awake for hours, biding his time until she came or didn't come.

Now she was there. He felt her presence though not her

166

flesh. She didn't speak. In moments, Cross heard the regular rhythms of her sleep. He took his pillow, grabbed a sheet and cotton blanket from the hall closet and went into the living room, settling himself on the sofa.

Moonlight slipped between the pines and set a pattern upon the walls and floors. There was a large world out there. Tomorrow, he would investigate it.

The City-County Building occupied a square block not far from the old City Market—a collection of booths selling fresh produce, cheese, and other sorts of things in what was no doubt an early mall concept. It was an old, one-story brick building.

Another, adjacent block was filled by the Marion County Jail, a blue brick building that, if it weren't for the gun-slit windows, looked like it belonged on Miami Beach.

The City-County building was a 26-story box. It wasn't particularly distinguished nor, in modern times, particularly tall.

The clean lines were obstructed inside by the old wooden desks, a litter of makeshift signs, and electronic gear to make sure you weren't bringing a bazooka to the courtrooms, the Mayor's office or any one of hundreds of city offices, including the police. The seventies modern building, at one time considered a skyscraper, was vastly different from the huge, regal domed state capitol building that housed similar bureaucracies for the state government.

In one innocuous room were Max Rafferty and Bradley Gray Pedersen—two people Shanahan didn't have much use for. For the most part Shanahan believed in a live and let live philosophy and the folks he didn't like didn't. The abuse of power, a disease that affects some cops, many politicians, and a number of those with extreme wealth, was a trait of character the detective couldn't abide.

Also in the room was James Fenimore Kowalski, who only had to cross the street to attend the meeting, and a slender dark-haired man in a black suit, white shirt, and pale-blue tie.

Shanahan assumed he was an assistant district attorney, an assumption that was validated by the man in a warm, friendly, respectful way.

They were seated at a conference table with Rafferty. Pedersen and an empty chair on one side and Kowalski on the other, with the D.A., Mark Lowe, at the head. Mark stood as Shanahan came in, but took his seat after they shook hands. Shanahan sat beside Kowalski.

Rafferty looked at Shanahan with a look that was difficult to decipher. Amusement maybe. That wasn't good.

"We're waiting for Mr. Pedersen's attorney," Mark Lowe said. "He called. He's parking his car at the moment. We'll give him a few minutes."

The air was conditioned. One could hear it rattling through the ventilation system. Still, it was stuffy inside the small conference room, and not particularly cool.

"In the meantime," Pedersen said, "I want to apologize to you, Mr. Shanahan. The restraining order was an overreaction. I hope you'll understand that my first thoughts were that if security could be so easily violated, who else might be there? It's not just that CEOs like me are periodically kidnapped for ransom, but we had several important people at the gathering, including a powerful US senator. I was worried and, I guess, angry. I hope you'll forgive me."

Shanahan was quiet for a moment. The small audience was expectant.

"It would be very bad mannered," Shanahan said, "for anyone not to accept the sincere apologies of someone else. Not that much harm was done."

"Thank you," Pedersen said, smiling.

Rafferty grinned. Kowalski looked perplexed. Lowe appeared stone-faced.

"One other thing," Pedersen went on, placing his hands on the table, joining them in such a way that church and steeple could be performed with little additional effort, or prayer, Shanahan thought. "I agreed to come down here because—who knows—maybe I know something that would be helpful.

I asked my attorney to join us when I learned that a polygraph test might also be helpful. I don't object to it, but having proprietary information that relates to my position as CEO of Noah Rose and Company, I need to be sure those interests are protected. Set limits, that's all."

Cross slept maybe two hours. It was difficult to tell. Up at dawn, he had been googling Ohio property records for Lester Channing. There were Channings around, none of them Lester. He found phone records in Cincinnati and made a note to call later in the morning.

Margot came in at ten thirty, gave him a faint smile on her way to the kitchen.

He wanted to say something, but he didn't know what to say. He was, for some reason, entirely neutral to the situation.

"I want you to know how much I appreciate your letting me stay here," she said. "I don't feel quite so lost."

It seemed far too early in the morning to have conversations like that.

"Not a problem." He wondered if he were lying. It was too early in the morning for that kind of thinking as well.

"It won't be much longer," she said. "I'm leaving the day of the race. I might be back in August for the Old Brickyard."

The Old Brickyard was another big race in the city. A different kind of auto race bringing in a different kind of fan. Where the Indianapolis 500 was an international race with high-performance cars, the NASCAR event was born in the southern US and brought with it a country-western flavor.

Cross didn't comment. He couldn't. He didn't know what he was feeling. Whatever it was, it wasn't pleasant.

"You all right?"

"Sure," he said, knowing full well she wasn't going to buy it.

"You want to go back to bed for awhile?" she asked.

"Do you want to?" he asked, but it was more of a challenge than an I-can't-believe-it "yes."

169

"Make you feel better," she said, unconvincingly. She hadn't pulled it off.

"Just because we know each other really well, doesn't mean we love each other."

"I know. I wasn't sure you knew."

Was sex always payment? An exchange of services?

"Sometimes business is pleasure," she said. "Look, we keep coming back to this. Just in different ways. We change the language, but it is the same game. And the game is fine by me. You have to figure out if it's fine by you."

It was true.

"Maybe, when you leave, that should be it," he said, not quite firmly.

"You know, I didn't exactly look you up this time."

"But you came over."

"You said you wanted me to."

"I didn't," he said.

"Oh yes you did. In the parking lot. Your eyes, your voice. There are many ways to communicate. I guess sometimes you just don't know what you're saying. Or what you want."

"There it is," he said. "Right on the money."

There she was. So sad. Too much sadness for the morning.

She dressed. When she left, he knew he'd never see her again. He didn't know how he felt about it.

Cross thought ahead. Tonight, he'd get a bottle of tequila and when night fell he'd put on Carlos Santana. "Black Magic Woman."

"You poor little baby," Cross said, fully comprehending his anticipated behavior.

"What?" Margot said, standing by the door.

"Nothing." In his mind, he was laughing.

She blew him a kiss.

"We'll both be fine," she said.

Even now, she knew what he was thinking.

Twenty-Three

A Mr. Sadler arrived. Gray suit jacket over the arm that carried the briefcase. Blue shirt, suspenders. He apologized, saying that even though he was late, he hoped that things could be wrapped up in an hour. His time, it seemed to Shanahan, was much more valuable than the others'.

"What was your relationship to Miss Lianna Bailey?" Kowalski asked.

"Boss. Employee."

"That cold?" Kowalski continued.

"No, of course not. We were very close. We talked about things not necessarily related to work. Her possible marriage. Her new home. But essentially, I operate a business. She was kind of my chief of staff, determining day-to-day priorities based on our mutual understanding of my goals for the company."

"Was there affection in your relationship?"

"Yes, as I alluded to. I liked her very much. But let's nip this little affair thing in the bud. I did not ever . . . ever . . . have an intimate relationship with Lianna Bailey. And if I might, in the interests of cutting to the chase, I know nothing of Miss Bailey's disappearance. If I did, I would tell you. I saw her at work the day of her disappearance. I was alarmed when I learned she did not show up the next day and did not call in."

"You called her at home."

"I didn't. Someone at Noah Rose and Company tried to reach her."

"How?"

171

"I don't know."

"Who?"

"Miss Schmidt possibly. She's the one who told me that there was a problem."

Lowe and Sadler remained quiet, listening with focus.

"And where were you on the night she disappeared?" Kowalski asked.

Shanahan knew he'd have an alibi. After all, a man in his position and with his resources would not personally engage in a kidnapping.

"I worked until eight that evening. I met my wife at eight thirty at a restaurant—the Element, I believe. We went home. I did some work in the study. Went to bed before eleven."

"Your wife can account for your hours?"

"I'm sure she can. Yes."

"I'd like to ask a question," Shanahan said. He wasn't sure it was permitted, but they didn't object. "Your past work involves gene injection, cloning, biological engineering. Right?"

Pedersen's attorney started to say something, but Pedersen patted his hand, suggesting he be quiet.

"Let me say," Pedersen said. "The work I do and have done in the past is related to the areas you mention. However, I will not go there with you. I said that earlier. I won't even take a baby step down that road."

"I was told the reason you left Mason Life Systems. It strikes me that your work and her disappearance could be related," Shanahan said.

Pedersen seemed amused. "Oh, Mr. Shanahan, I wish you would tell me more. Who said what for a start. It's quite possible that this would mean a substantial additional settlement from my old alma mater. We signed confidentiality agreements, Mr. Shanahan. I still own thirty-three percent of the company. If they broke the agreement, I'd own twice that. You care to continue? And if it came from a person no longer employed, I'd take that person for everything he or she owns, plus ruin his life forever—professionally speaking. So I don't think anyone is going to back your contention."

"Do you have any more questions that relate to the disappearance?" Sadler asked.

"You know nothing, absolutely nothing about her disappearance?" Kowalski asked.

"No."

"You have no thoughts about it?"

"I surely wish I did. I miss her personally and professionally."

"Mr. Pedersen," Lowe the D.A. finally said, "you've consented to a polygraph. We have it set up in the other room." Everyone stood. "There will be no audience, I'm afraid. However, a full, detailed report will be available to you Mr. Kowalski."

Rafferty grinned as they all left the room.

Waiting for the elevator, Kowalski told Shanahan that the odds were that even if Pedersen were lying it wouldn't matter.

"A lie detector measures stress," Kowalski said. "My guess is that Pedersen isn't easily stressed."

"So what he's doing is taking himself off the list of suspects?" Shanahan said.

"Yes, and we just barely got him on that list. Unfortunately, it is a list of one. Now, that's what I call a short list."

"Channing's on the list," Shanahan said. "Who knows? In the end, maybe he did it all. For his own reasons. Not as a surrogate for someone else."

"You believe that?"

"So far, what I believe hasn't gotten us anywhere. I think we find out what Channing's connections are to Lianna Bailey."

"Sounds like a job for a private investigator," Kowalski said.

"Or two."

The taxi arrived. She was out the door, carrying a small bag. He checked the room. He wanted to be sure that he was right— that she wasn't coming back. He had his hunch verified. Not a shoe, or a pair of panties, or a hairbrush. Just a few cigarette stubs. He was emptying those when the phone rang.

Cross invited Shanahan over. Promised him a cup of coffee and an important announcement about his life.

173

"Can't wait," Shanahan told him. "The war in the Middle East and your life. Keeps me on edge."

Shanahan drove by the Channing residence. The van was still in front. Shanahan knocked on the screen door. He could see two women busy putting things in paper bags. A woman looking a bit like Mrs. Channing answered.

"Mrs. Channing, please."

The other woman looked up, recognized Shanahan, came to the door.

"Do you know anything?"

"I was about to ask you the same question," Shanahan said.

"No. And I don't think I care," she said. Her eyes looked better. She hadn't cried recently. "I'm getting on with my life."

Shanahan pulled out his small notebook, wrote his name and phone number on a blank page, tore it out, and handed it to Mrs. Channing.

"If he contacts you, let me know. As I said earlier, we're trying to find a missing woman. We know he's connected."

"Another affair? What's new?" she said.

"Maybe more serious than that," Shanahan said, though maybe, he thought, Mrs. Channing wouldn't see it that way.

Next stop, Universal Security. A thin elderly man, with bottle lens glasses, sat at a battered wooden desk facing the door. On his desk were a vintage computer, a telephone, and a couple of large ledger-type books. He didn't smile. He didn't offer a "May I help you?"

He looked up grudgingly.

"Lester Channing," Shanahan said.

"Can't help you there," the man said.

"Why?" Shanahan fished.

"Not around."

"When will he be back?"

"That's the 64,000-dollar question."

Shanahan showed the man his ID. The man was obviously unimpressed. He just kept looking, like he expected something intelligible to come out of the old detective's lips.

"Let's put it this way. There's a criminal investigation going on. There's a lady missing, and there's Channing missing and I'm hoping to find him."

"That'd be a blessing," the man said.

"Because he owes you money, right?"

"No, he don't. I took my money. But next week I'd have to work for free."

"So help me."

"I don't know where he went. He didn't say. He said he'd be gone a couple of days and a couple of days have come and gone."

"You can still help," Shanahan said.

"Go on."

"How about a client list? Going back maybe a couple of years."

"Won't take long."

"We do a lot of the security for night clubs, mostly strip clubs. We provide bouncers, parking lot security, that sort of thing."

"Nobody else."

"Nothing long term," the man said, opening up one of the ledgers. He took out a tablet with legal-sized, lined yellow paper. He plucked a pencil from a coffee cup filled with various instruments of writing, and began scribing.

Shanahan asked the man about Channing's habits, hang-outs, friends. The only thing he got that was helpful was the list. And depending on how you looked at it, the list wasn't helpful at all.

The Palace of Gold strip club was on the list as were a dozen or so other clubs, rock clubs, dance clubs and strip clubs. Unfortunately so were a few more respectable companies, including Masters, Credlin and Hawkins, the investment firm that employed Todd Evans. Shanahan looked for Noah Rose & Company. Not there. There were a couple of shopping malls, a discount store chain, and a company called Scepter Lines, Inc. A trucking company?

Could the Masters, Credlin and Hawkins link simply be a

175

coincidence? Shanahan doubted it, but he'd try to hold back the obvious suspicion and betrayal he felt. Some things that were obvious were irrelevant. He wanted to believe that, anyway.

"So I'm pretty sure I'm going to go gay," Cross said.

"A person can do that?" Shanahan asked, closing the door behind him. "Just like that. Just change orientation."

"This heterosexual thing just isn't working," Cross said. "I mean all the ministers say it's a choice, you know. So apparently one day I chose to be heterosexual. I don't remember that day. But one day I must have. Maybe sometime in the third grade I looked at little Bobby Granville and then at Linda Lee and I chose Linda Lee. But, maybe it was the wrong choice."

"I see." Shanahan wouldn't bite. "Good luck."

"This isn't easy," Cross said. "I don't know what my type is—in males, I mean. This is all so new to me."

"I hope it's not older men."

"I know what it's not. No male strippers."

"I suppose that's wise."

"No Chippendales," Cross said. "Definitely no Chippendales."

"I thought Chip and Dale were gophers."

"They were male gophers. Coffee?"

"I thought you'd never ask."

"What do we do now?" Cross shouted from the kitchen.

Shanahan went in. "We find Channing and we find Channing's connection to Lianna Bailey. Maybe Channing is the one and only."

"You believe that."

"About as much as I believe you're going to find the man of your dreams." He didn't want to drain Cross of any energy in the pursuit of Channing by suggesting that there was a potential connection between Channing and Evans. He wanted to talk with Evans first. After all, there were a couple of other legitimate companies on the list.

"Yeah," Cross said. "You're right, it's probably not any easier being gay. So, celibacy, here I come."

176

Cross explained what he'd learned earlier in the morning, before Margot's exit. He found Channing's mother in Cincinnati. She hadn't heard from him since Christmas. Not unusual. It was the way he was, she said. Channing's father was no longer alive. He had no siblings. The elder Mrs. Channing had no idea if her son had friends in the area. He had spent little time there, she said, since he left years ago.

"The only other bit of information she could provide was that he was an avid hunter and would sometimes hunt in the area. Some woods somewhere. She thought she remembered he owned some land."

"Cooperative," Shanahan said.

"I told her he'd been gone awhile and some of the guys at work were concerned."

"Have you had a chance to find anything?"

"Before my latest love catastrophe arose this A.M., I checked Ohio property tax records by computer and by phone. Nothing listed under Lester Channing," Cross said.

"Indiana," Shanahan said. "Cincinnati is so close to the line. You don't even have to cross a river. And, if I recall, there are areas where there's not a lot of population in that part of the state."

"And Kentucky," Cross said, "which is just across the river from Cincinnati. I'll work on it this afternoon. Channing's not making it easy."

"He might not even own the land anymore."

"Damn." Cross was having a Eureka moment.

"What?"

"Channing as much as told me he had some property, but that his retirement plans changed. He wanted to go some place warm."

"Go for it," Shanahan said. He felt bad about not filling him in completely on the Evans Universal connection. He'd work better, perhaps, if he didn't know. Most people, probably even most lawyers, would prefer to work for defendants who, in fact, are innocent, and not just trying to beat the system. Certainly that's how Shanahan felt.

177

Twenty-Four

S hanahan was beginning to feel like a taxi driver, moving from one place to another. He was straining the no doubt meager reserves of his classic, but not classic-looking, 1976 Chevy Malibu. It had 190,000 miles on a car built to self-destruct much earlier than that. Not a Volvo or even a Subaru, it nonetheless sputtered along. Perhaps it was a race between man and machine—to see which one outlived the other.

A phone would have been easier, but Shanahan was uncomfortable on the phone. He always preferred face to face when possible. But it was clear he should have phoned ahead. Kowalski's office was closed. Probably in court. He did have other clients, Shanahan presumed.

Shanahan stopped for gas and headed out to Ravenswood. He hadn't been paying attention to the weather reports lately, and didn't notice until he was gassing up that the sky had darkened and there was the slightest coolness that accompanied something a little more than a spring breeze. Storm maybe. Shanahan thought of the race, just days away. He hoped it would jeopardize Indianapolis's day in the international sun. It is the only way the world knew of its existence and Shanahan, surprising himself, always felt a little tug of loyalty to the city that he, by sheer happenstance, called home.

Halfway to Ravenswood, the sky broke. Torrents of rain overpowered the decades-old machine that moved his windshield wipers. He had to pull off the road briefly, until the worst had past.

He hoped Maureen had shut the windows. There was a sudden flash of light, then deep, growling thunder. Not usually one to look on the bright side, he was glad it was a storm and not a tornado.

The crops could use the rain, he thought, taking him back to his father's predictable comment every time a drop fell from the sky. There were times the crops didn't need the rain, but he would never correct his father. He couldn't see out at all, just the water rolling down the windows. He reclined his seat slightly, put his head back, closed his eyes. It might be awhile. The sound of the rain on the metal roof was hypnotic.

He opened his eyes. He was on a bunk. Rain pummeled the corrugated steel roof above him. There must have been two, maybe three dozen bunk beds, all empty. He wore olive drab boxer shorts. He looked down, one of his legs—at the calf. It was bandaged. Some blood had soaked through. Next to him was an envelope. No mistaking it, made of thin paper. An airmail envelope. There was a sheet of paper with blue ink sentences. A photograph. A child. A baby. He picked up the letter. He tried to read it. It made no sense. He was long past all of that. Wasn't he? Why did he have to go back? He didn't want to be there. He tried to scream. There was no sound coming from his lips. He had to get out of there. He had to wake up. He tried to open his eyes. At first, he didn't think he could open them, but there was a sliver of light. Slowly, the sliver expanded. Open, he gasped for breath. He was awake. Whatever it was receded. Wherever he had been drifted back where it came from.

He was awake. The rain had stopped. He looked at his watch. Two hours had passed. He didn't feel rested. Instead, he felt he'd traveled a day or two in a horse-drawn wagon. He brought his seat forward, started the engine. It was mid-afternoon. The loss of time seemed worse in light of the possibility that she was still alive and awaiting discovery.

Evans was there. Kowalski wasn't.

The young man, in cotton pants, a T-shirt, and socks, stepped aside so Shanahan could come in. Perhaps he too had napped.

179

His eyelids looked heavy. His face was expressionless.

"How are you enjoying your stay?"

"A bit antsy," Evans said. "He has a lot of books. There's television. I feel so worthless. Just waiting. Not doing anything to find her."

"You could be more helpful," Shanahan said, not sure if he'd buried the anger or not. It appeared he hadn't.

Evans looked surprised and hurt. "I'm willing," he said defensively.

"You said you didn't know Lester Channing."

"That's right. I don't."

"Lester Channing's firm, Universal Security, did work for your employer."

Evans's shrug meant "so what?"

"It's pretty far-fetched to think it's coincidence that among the very few main-street kind of companies that his company worked for is the one that employed the prime suspect of a murder with which we know Lester was involved."

Evans looked worried. "I don't know what to say."

"You had nothing to do with hiring Universal Security."

"That's not my job."

"Why would your company hire a security firm?"

"The only time I know of is the annual meeting and reception. We have a few security people make sure there are no gatecrashers, that the party doesn't get out of hand. Just a handful of security guards for a few hours every year as far as I know."

"And that was what Universal Security was hired to do?"

"I'm guessing. I don't remember the name of the security firm."

"Who attends these receptions?"

"Our most valued customers, our firm's staff and board of directors. It's mostly business."

"Who else?"

"That's it."

"Spouses invited?"

"Yes, I forgot that. Yes. Friends sometimes, and spouses. Spouses are desirable."

"Did Lianna go to these events?"

"Yes," he said, suddenly moving from defense to interest. "Yes, she always came."

It seemed that no matter how much evidence pointed at Todd Evans, the young man came up with a way to render it tentative, uncertain. Only, this time Shanahan was the one who came up with the counter arguments. Was Evans that good?

"Who can get me the list of folks welcomed that evening?"

"Mr. Credlin's secretary," Evans said. "She sends out the invitations and manages the event."

"Who would have hired the security guards?"

"Mr. Credlin's secretary. Her name is Mrs. Collins."

Cross ran into a dead end. Past property owner records and transactions were not accessible by computer. In a desperate attempt, he typed in Universal Security. Nothing. As a shot in the dark, he typed in Noah Rose & Company. Nothing.

It was possible, he supposed, to traipse through the records of ownership for all counties in the proximity of the Indiana, Ohio, Kentucky state lines either at some county clerk's office or perhaps state files. But he couldn't convince himself that it was worthwhile. Even if he could spend the hours on this, there was no guarantee that any answers were buried there.

Shanahan sat in the lobby of Masters, Credlin and Hawkins, waiting for someone to fetch him. It was a comfortable place. There was an adjacent room with computers on tables high enough for people to stand and key in, presumably to check on stock prices. An electronic ticker tape moved across a screen mounted on one wall of the lobby. It was all gibberish to Shanahan.

The fetcher was Mrs. Collins, herself—a pleasant woman who looked to be someone's kindly aunt. She smiled. He stood.

"Thank you for meeting with me," Shanahan said.

"I hope I can help. I can't believe Todd would be involved in anything like this. You said on the phone you needed some kind of list."

"Yes, I would like the guest list to your annual meeting and reception, whatever that's called."

"Last year's?"

"Any year that Universal Security provided you with guards."

"That would be last year."

"First year they worked for you?"

"And last. They were a little . . . uh . . . rugged for our clientele. I don't mean they hurt anyone or anything. Just a little rough around the edges. They didn't seem to understand what it was they were hired to do."

"I don't want to take up too much of your time. Is it possible for me to see the list?"

"If you don't mind waiting a few minutes, I can do it now." She turned to go, but stopped and turned back to him. "These are our clients," she said, suddenly looking a bit apprehensive.

"I promise you I'm not working for the competition. Universal Security is tied to the disappearance of Lianna Bailey and Lianna Bailey is tied to Todd Evans."

"All right," she said, but she didn't seem fully convinced. "You promise, right? I mean, you'll keep all of this to yourself?"

"I will."

She seemed to have worked it out by the time she returned. There were at least twenty pages, each with twenty or so names, some of them asterisked and some of them checked and others lined out. Still others were without marks or notations. There were a couple of names written in at the end.

This wasn't a copy. It was the original. He knew he wasn't going to get to walk out of there with the names.

"The checks mean they showed up," she said. "If they're lined out, that means they cancelled. If they're written in, that means they were approved on the spot. The asterisks mean they are either very rich or very powerful or both."

"And if there's nothing?"

"They didn't show up, but didn't formally cancel," she said.

"We thought it best if you review it here. You're free to make notes."

"I know," he said. He wasn't sure if the use of "we" was used to take the sting out of the more egoist "I," or whether she had conferred with someone. Didn't matter. He'd have to make the best of it.

He sat back down on the comfortable leather chair and she sat down across from him, picked up a *Fortune* magazine from the table and thumbed through as Shanahan began to scan the list.

He had hoped to find Pedersen's name and skipped to the Ps only to find there was a Peterson and a Petrovski, but not the name he wanted. He flipped back to page one and began.

He recognized a few names, but none of them seemed relevant. Lianna Bailey was listed. In parentheses behind it was "guest, T. E."

"So staff could bring guests?" he asked Mrs. Collins.

"Oh yes. Lianna was here that night."

"Did she talk to anybody?"

"I wouldn't know. I was busy trying to make sure the food trays were replenished, the bartenders didn't run out of vodka—that sort of thing."

Shanahan let his eyes travel down page one, two. Nothing. He was nearly done with the machine-printed names and began looking at the half a dozen handwritten names.

He recognized one right away. Mary Beth Schmidt. Next to it, in parentheses, was noted "guest, T. E." Again, not a surprise, she was Lianna's closest friend.

That was it. He wished he could take the list with him. Perhaps someone else could make something of it.

"Do you know if Mr. Lester Channing was there that night?"

"Yes, I do know, because we exchanged words several times during the evening."

"What about?"

"About the uniforms and about his guards mingling with the guests."

"Nibbling on canapés is not in the job description?"

"No."

"Did he take the criticism well?" Shanahan asked.

"He told his guards to behave themselves, but thought the rules didn't apply to him. I found him chatting up the guests periodically throughout the evening. I think he was trying to drum up business."

"Thank you Mrs. Collins."

"Were we able to help?"

"Maybe. I don't know yet. But I do appreciate your time."

Shanahan huddled over the spot of light pooled on his desk from the lamp. He scribbled on the small pages of his notebook. He listed the possible motives for Lianna's disappearance and the corresponding abductor or murderer:

Jealousy, anger, domestic conflict: Todd Evans.

Predator, sexual thrills: Lester Channing or unknown.

Prevent embarrassment, protect investment, reputation: Bradley Gray Pedersen.

That's when the list stopped. It was a small circle, seemingly growing smaller. An earlier call from Kowalski provided disappointing news. Pedersen passed the polygraph without question. It wasn't even "inconclusive." As Cross said, it was possible for a guy like Pedersen to beat it. He was smart, calm, confident.

Maureen was on the sofa, eyes focused on the screen of her laptop computer. He knew what she was doing. She was focused on where to get the best pasta, not his dark thoughts.

The sun had disappeared so subtly that no one had bothered to turn on more lights.

"Do you want to do three cities and the coast?" she asked, looking up, the color from the computer screen flashing a pattern of various colors on her face. "Or do you think we could squeeze in four? All that I've read says we don't need to spend more than a couple of days in Venice."

"Why don't you put a couple of itineraries together and we can go over them."

"I like that," she said. "All right, what are you up to?"

Shanahan read her the list he'd jotted down.

"Such a chauvinist. No women on your list? What's the matter? You don't think women are equal to men when it comes to murder?"

"What?"

"She had a sister, right?"

"Jasmine." Shanahan shrugged. He didn't see their obvious sibling rivalry leading to anything drastic. But he wrote it down anyway. Jealousy, explosive argument: Jasmine Bailey.

"All right."

"And what about that woman you interviewed. Her best friend?"

"Mary Beth Schmidt. I don't know what kind of motive she would have. They were friends, Mary Beth had to assume some of her duties."

"Maybe there was a little love quadrangle. Your Mr. Pedersen, his wife, Lianna, and Mary."

"If you don't mind leaving Italy for a moment and return to little old Indiana, do your stuff on the computer with Mary Beth Schmidt."

Shanahan stood, turned on a light near the sofa. The room had been starkly dark and depressing. Now, the shadows seemed ominous. He turned on another light near the upholstered chair, before going into the kitchen to find a roast chicken leg and a bottle of Miller beer. He gave Maureen a few minutes to find a new set of coordinates in the virtual universe.

"There are several items," Maureen said, as Shanahan came back into the living room. "Something connected with Mason Life Systems. An interview with a magazine or something."

"Go on."

"OK, another when she was appointed to Executive Vice President of Operations for Noah Rose and Company."

"More?"

"Oh yes, there maybe pages and pages. Looks like she was a co-author on a book, *Human Cloning—Devils and Angels*."

"Don't lose track of that one, but keep going," Shanahan said. He moved in beside her but couldn't read anything.

185

"Here's one," Maureen said. "Interesting. It's something about medical laboratory construction 'for the new age in genetics, cloning, and other strange but alluring bio-technology.'"

"Hold on to that one too," Shanahan said.

"No wait, it says 'Mary Beth Schmidt, Scepter Bio Lines CEO.' Could this be another Mary Beth Schmidt?"

"That would be a helluva coincidence. Why don't you open that one?"

Twenty-Five

C ross sat on the sofa, feeling as if he were in a hospital
waiting room, waiting for information before he could
go home and get about his life. He had no notion of what to
do, what he wanted to do, or needed to do. He was absolutely
without motivation. Not a thing in the world would thrill him.
He wasn't sure, but he thought not a thing in the world would
disturb him, make him happy or make him sad.

Blank, blank, blank.

"Bingo," Shanahan said, now sitting beside Maureen and reading. His eyes raced over the text. In the last paragraph, the
copy revealed that Scepter was a subsidiary of Noah Rose &
Company, and that it came into existence three years ago. The
subsidiary developed prefab labs. "Installed in thirty days in
either existing structures or as a new structure."

"Why is this Bingo?" Maureen asked.

"Scepter was a client of Universal Security."

"And?"

"Channing and Mary Beth."

"I never liked her," Maureen said.

Shanahan went to the phone, called Cross.

"The name to look up on the property records. Scepter Bio
Lines."

"Just what I needed," Cross said. "A little direction."

He found it. It was 2 A.M. Sober, decaffeinated, alert and five
hours after he started, he found Scepter Bio Lines owning 127
acres of land in Ripley County. Ripley was close enough—in

the middle of a triangle with the points being Indianapolis, Cincinnati and Louisville. Somewhere near Laughery Creek and the Fish and Wild Life Area.

"Damn," Cross said. All it took, he thought, was a little victory to lift him from his somnambulist state of mind. His mind raced, but it ended up back where it started. What was the connection?

He called Shanahan.

"We're going to Versailles," Cross said into the phone after hearing a soggy hello.

"Is this the gay thing again?" Shanahan asked.

"No."

"Well Maureen wants to go to Italy, not France."

"Milan is nearby."

"What are you doing? Are you drunk?" Shanahan asked.

"Scepter owns a hundred or so acres in Ripley County, somewhere near Versailles."

There was a lengthy quiet.

"Shanahan?" Cross asked, thinking the person on the other end of the line might have fallen back asleep.

"Remind me, because I think this fits too well. Didn't you tell me the Channings came from Cincinnati?"

"I did."

"We're somewhere now," said Shanahan. "Let me call you back from the kitchen. I'll tell you all about it."

"We need to be able to leave in an hour. It's three o'clock now," Shanahan said, wide awake. "If we leave at four we'll get down there by five. We can grab coffee, breakfast maybe, and get to the property before first light."

"Why not just call the police?" Cross asked.

Einstein came into the kitchen, seemingly perplexed by the activity. Night in the house belonged to him. He didn't like it.

"I'd rather poke around first, make sure."

Now it was Maureen who came in, half-asleep, not sure if she were curious or merely perplexed.

"I'll pick you up at four," Shanahan said. "Wear boots, clothes you'd wear tromping around the woods. Bring a weapon, if you have one."

"That's a lot of area to cover," Cross said.

"I know. Will your cell phone work over there?"

"If we're not in a tunnel, probably."

"Bring it," Shanahan said. He put the phone back in the cradle.

"What's up?" Maureen asked, eyes squinting in the kitchen light.

"Going on a little trip," he said.

"Where?"

"Versailles."

"The palace of?"

"Maybe there's a palace there. Who knows?"

"You know where she is?"

"I think so."

There were four of them in the car. Shanahan drove. Maureen was beside him. Cross was in the back seat with Casey. No one spoke. A combination of interrupted sleep, anxiety, and the darkness conspired to keep things quiet. Casey slept. Maureen stared out of the window, though it was doubtful she could see anything. Cross leaned back, his head thrown back. Shanahan followed the headlights on the wet pavement. He could see little of the land they passed through.

Occasionally, an oncoming car would flash sudden, harsh, and unflattering light into the car. A bug would splat against the windshield. There was no sound but the hum of the old engine and a steady hiss as air leaked in the window on the passenger side, a window that no longer closed as tight as it once did. The rain had cooled things off for awhile, but the warm humid air was returning and it was difficult to decide whether to keep the windows up or down.

Once they reached Versailles and off Highway 421 to the back roads, it was Maureen's job to navigate. With a flashlight on the map, they had gone from Interstate to four-lane highway to two-way highway to gravel roads. All at night, with Shanahan carefully calculating curves. It was desolate and if there was anyone up anywhere he was sure this old car roaming these old secondary roads would be highly suspicious.

They had seen no diners open, no lights anywhere, as they passed through a sleepy Versailles. But now the light was coming. And if the map were correct and the mile markers were correct, they had found the fence that marked the land now belonging to Scepter Bio Lines. There was enough light now to read the signs: PRIVATE PROPERTY, KEEP OUT, NO HUNTING/NO FISHING, TRESPASSERS WILL BE PROSECUTED. Someone had spray-painted EX over the PROS.

They drove the perimeter looking for an entrance. But it was difficult to tell where all of the boundaries were. The only one they could be sure of was the one where the mile markers matched.

Shanahan parked on the shoulder across the road. Everyone piled out. Casey and Cross both went to answer the call of nature in their own ways. Shanahan retrieved metal cutters from the trunk as well as his old Army .45 and a pair of binoculars. He desperately wished he didn't have to use it. Not only did he hate guns, he wasn't sure his worn old body could stand the powerful kick of the .45.

He cut through the relatively new chain-link fence as Maureen focused the flashlight on his work. Cross rubbed his eyes. Shanahan peeled back the fence, allowing Maureen, then Casey, then Cross, then himself, to crawl through. Woods were in front of them. How to canvas 127 acres of wooded land was a problem. If they fanned out, they'd easily become lost. If they tracked through together, they risked traveling in circles.

They went in, Shanahan hoping that luck would be on their side. The ground was soggy. It had rained there too and the water had cooled the earth. But the air was warmer now, and steam rose up a foot or more from the damp ground, giving the whole scene an eerie, colorless, dawn of the dead feeling. They had walked twenty minutes or so when they came upon a stream. Just what he wanted. If there were any structure built on this land, it would seem likely they would put it at least somewhat close to water—either for the view or for its potential practical application.

The stream was clear and moving rapidly over rocks and twigs and branches—no doubt energized by the earlier rain. The earth gave beneath their feet as they walked along beside it. Casey walked along with them for awhile, then darted away, having caught a wild scent. Shanahan wanted to call him, but didn't want to make noise. He wasn't sure how close they were to wherever it was they were going. He wished he'd been smarter and put his occasionally recalcitrant hound on a leash. But in moments, Casey returned. He moved ahead of them now as a little more light began to seep into the woods. The four of them reached a point where it appeared that others had walked along here—a muddy path with hints of shoeprints. Perhaps they were getting close. Perhaps not.

Shanahan felt for the .45. It was still there. The weight in his jacket pocket should have been enough reassurance, but it wasn't. He thought he knew what he'd find, but there were no guarantees. And certainly, his hunches had been wrong before. Maybe nothing would happen. Maybe this was a wild-goose chase, which is why he hadn't called Lt. Swann. But he had Swann's phone number, and Cross had his cell phone.

Five slow minutes ahead, there was an outbuilding. It had been there for years and leaned heavily to one side. Casey was the first to examine it. Nothing there. Hadn't been in quite awhile. However, there was a broader path that now left the stream and headed to the left. It had been a gravel path at one time, but there was only a scattering of gravel there now.

New choices. What was it that Yogi Berra said? If you come to a fork in the road, take it. Should they split up? The path could lead nowhere. Or it could be the stream led nowhere. Perhaps both.

"You have a gun?" Shanahan asked Cross.

He nodded. "I'll take the babbling brook. Why don't you take the path?"

"OK."

"Stay behind me, please, maybe twenty feet," Shanahan said. "Not because you are a woman," he added when he saw the scowl form on her face, "but because I have the .45."

She smiled, nodded. She bowed and swept her arm in an exaggerated motion of a gallant "after you."

Casey raced ahead, then stopped, looked back, waiting for the slow-moving humans to catch up.

Cross was glad to be alone. In a few minutes, he began to feel exhilarated, completely absorbed by nature, senses sharpened. There were moments years ago when he was a cop that he felt this kind of sensation. It felt good. He felt alive in ways he hadn't felt for a long time.

The stream gradually angled in. He found himself slowly heading in the same direction that Shanahan and entourage had gone. Something moved quickly through the brush beside him. Cross couldn't tell what it was. In this part of the country he didn't have to worry about bears or mountain lions. The only predator likely to be lurking in these woods was Channing. Cross believed Channing wouldn't hesitate to kill him. He might already be a murderer with little to lose.

Shanahan walked on the edge of the path so that he could slip into the woods if need be. He'd already motioned for Maureen to do the same. The path seemed to be gradually going right, so they walked on the right side of it, in order to minimize visibility from anyone ahead. About ten minutes into the walk Shanahan saw the building. He stopped and moved into the woods, moving through the trees toward the structure. He wanted to look at it carefully, but he didn't want to be seen looking at it.

He heard movement behind him, and saw Maureen slipping in behind him. The building—a cabin really—seemed perfectly suited to the environment. The roof seemed in good condition. The windows, dirty as they were, were unbroken. The siding was comprised of thin slats of weathered wood. The door was on one of the other sides. He lifted the binoculars and tried to see through the windows. But he saw nothing. It was lighter outside than inside, barely. He'd have to get up close.

"Stay here," he whispered. "Keep Casey." But the dog had already wandered off. He handed her the binoculars.

Shanahan made his way to the edge of the woods and then moved across the ten feet or so between the trees and the cabin.

He pressed himself against the building, moving slowly toward the window on the far left. He shielded his eyes, pressed his nose against the glance. It was a bedroom. There was a quilt askew on a bed that had sheets. There was a jacket hanging on the doorknob. The door was partially open. Shanahan was pretty sure someone was living there.

Twenty-Six

The path along the stream narrowed, then ceased to exist, though the stream itself went on. Realizing he could not go on without traipsing back into the woods, where he could easily get lost, he stood a moment to think about a plan.

There were a few choices. He could walk in the stream. He could walk in the woods, but keep the stream to his right, hoping it would eventually lead somewhere. Or, he could retrace his steps, go back to the path that the others had taken and try to catch up with them.

He decided on the third. Knowing his way, and knowing the terrain, he traversed the space back more quickly.

Cross heard the twigs crack, heard something large moving through the brush. It was sudden. He pulled out his .38, and had it ready before he saw the young deer who peered at him curiously before bounding away.

Shanahan ducked under the window and moved around the cabin. He soon saw the clearing where a battered blue Toyota pickup truck was parked. He could see the dirt road that came into the cabin and the front door.

As he turned the corner, he saw him. Channing had a hunting rifle of enough caliber that it would blow something like a rabbit or squirrel apart.

He held it low, but at this range, he wouldn't miss if he chose to fire.

"Where's Cross?" Channing asked. He recognized Shanahan from San Francisco.

"He has a different babysitter now."

"Don't be cute."

"Where's Lianna?" Shanahan asked.

Channing shook his head. "How did you find me?"

"Scepter Bio Lines."

Channing's eyes widened. Shanahan knew more than Channing had imagined and it changed things. He was recalculating. Shanahan hoped Channing would realize that the game was over. "You haven't killed her yet, have you?" Shanahan asked in as friendly a way as possible.

Channing wouldn't answer. "You think that I'm the only one who knows?" Shanahan asked. "You kill me and that's just one more crime you've committed."

"I'm not sure it matters, old man. I've done enough. And I'm kind of a gambler. You know? I'm used to betting against the odds."

"Doesn't look like you've won too many hands, now does it?"

Channing smiled. "You're a cocky old bastard."

Shanahan worried that Maureen might wander into this whole mess. Talking about the odds, Shanahan thought, it was more likely than not that Maureen would interfere and put her life in danger.

"She here?"

"Who?"

"Lianna."

Channing grinned wide, pretended to look around. Shrugged his shoulders. "I don't see her."

"What did you get out of this? Scepter willing to pay you that much?"

"You're awfully calm. Who else is out there? Cross?" He glanced around nervously. "Let's get inside."

Just then, Casey appeared.

"What the hell is that?"

"That's a Catahoula. Leopard dog."

The dog growled. It was low growl.

"I don't like shooting dogs," Channing said. "But I will."
"Let's go in, leave him out here."
"Not sure about that."
"You think he's got a cell phone?"
Channing smirked. They went inside.

Cross saw Casey cut back into the woods. As he approached the spot, he saw the corner of the cabin and decided to follow the dog. He startled her.

"Shhh," she whispered. "Shanahan went toward the cabin, then around to the other side."

Cross settled down in the low brush beside her. He borrowed the binoculars. They didn't provide anything that he couldn't see with naked eyes.

"How long has he been gone?" he said softly.

"Five minutes," she said. "Casey went too, but came back."

"That's a puzzle. Which side did he go around?"

"Left."

"OK, here's my cell phone. Call the Cavalry if I'm not back in ten."

Cross slipped out of the woods, going to his left, and moving around the other side of the house.

Shanahan sat on an uncomfortable ladder-back chair off to one side, but facing inside. Channing sat, rifle on his lap, in a battered leather chair facing him, taking an occasional deep breath. Shanahan's .45 was in his right hand.

"You don't have many options," Shanahan said. "Run and you'll be running forever."

Channing laughed. "I'll always be looking over my shoulder, right?"

"Right."

"What's my life going to be like in prison? I was a cop. You think that's better? I don't. And if you're not around it's only that bird's word against mine."

"Maybe you can get some points by turning yourself in. You haven't killed anybody, or have you?"

Channing didn't answer.

"If you did . . ."

"If I did, you're toast," Channing said. "What would I have to lose?"

"I've already told the police about your involvement. They have a signed statement from your friend at the Palace of Gold. You're implicated. In fact, there's an APB out on you. Not sure you could get out of the state."

"I can walk out of the state. It's only a few miles to Ohio."

"Kidnapping is a federal crime. State lines don't really mean a hell of a lot."

"Neither do you. You died in a hunting accident, your old hunting dog standing by the corpse. Convincing picture."

"Won't work," said Howie Cross who appeared from the hallway, a pistol in his hand, aimed at Channing. "You gotta know I'm in the mood to hurt you really bad. My kidneys still hurt."

Channing looked at Cross as he moved around in front. Cross plucked the .45 from Channing's hand and handed it to Shanahan. He did the same with the rifle. Shanahan put the .45 in his pocket, unloaded the rifle, and leaned it in a corner.

"You know why it wouldn't work?" Cross asked Channing.

"Oh tell me. You know you want to."

"We know who you're working for," Cross said.

"We know what this is all about. And so do the police," Shanahan added.

"You'll never get your money," Cross said. "Or a chance to spend it for that matter."

Channing's face showed both interest and wariness. Was he being tricked?

"Keep him in one place," Shanahan told Howie. "I want to look around."

Shanahan went to inspect the other rooms.

"You should lock your windows. Wide open," Cross told Channing.

"It's hot. No air-conditioning." He smirked.

"Where's Lianna?"

197

"I have no idea. I came out here to chill out, rest, do a little hunting," Channing said.

Shanahan came back in the room.

"Where's the entrance?" Shanahan asked.

"What are you talking about?"

"The lab."

"Are you talking about a dog?" Channing asked.

"I don't believe in torture," Cross said, "I want to clue you in on something. I'm not a practicing Christian. I don't believe in turning the other cheek."

Channing was thinking.

"It's over," Cross said.

"We'll find it. Or the police will," Shanahan said. "It's somewhere on this plot of land. We know that."

"Good for you."

"What happens if we take you and your partner away? Does that change anything?" Shanahan asked.

"What the Sam Hell are you talking about?"

"I mean you two are gone for awhile. Days pass. Weeks. Months. Does that change the crime you committed?" Shanahan asked.

Channing's eyes searched for something.

"Let me put it in a more positive way," Shanahan continued. "We're not really interested in you. We are interested in finding Lianna Bailey."

"Go on," Channing said.

"We're not the police. We've been hired to clear Todd Evans of her murder. If we find her alive . . . well, the rest is obvious."

"You mean you'd let me walk?" Channing said.

Cross looked confused for a moment, then nodded.

"We can let you drive. That your truck out there?" Shanahan asked.

"Yep. It is."

"Here's the deal. Cross here has a cell phone. In just a few moments he is either going to place a call to the police for your arrest. And then the folks will search the woods and find

. . . something. Or, you can take us to Lianna and while we're getting ready to take her home, you drive off into the sunset and live happily ever after."

"Now we have a discussion going," Channing said, standing. "This is good." He paced a few feet under Cross's watchful eye. "OK. I need my coat." Cross pulled it from the doorknob of the closet, felt for weapons, found an electronic key device in the pocket. That was it. He put it back and handed the jacket to Channing.

"C'mon," Channing said.

"Wait, wait, wait," Shanahan said. He walked to Channing and patted him down. Wallet, change, more keys. Not even a pocket knife.

"Hey, we have a deal," Channing objected.

"Life is so unfair," Cross said.

Channing walked out the door, followed at about three paces by Cross. Shanahan patted his jacket pocket for the .45 to reassure himself. It was there.

The three of them walked across the clearing in front of the cabin, shoes crunching against the gravel, to an opening in the woods, a wide path, also gravel. Within twenty feet, they could see the building, aluminum faced, but dulled by some additive.

It wouldn't have taken an army to find the place. Shanahan felt a little foolish bargaining for directions he could have found in five minutes. Once they arrived at the sliding doors it was apparent. Channing was necessary. There was a keypad, indicating that one must know the combination. As it turned out, it was more complicated than knowing a series of numbers. There was a pad by the numbers where Channing placed the index finger of his right hand. The doors slid open. Cross stepped into the small entry room where another door seemingly required a code. Channing went in, followed by Shanahan. There was a row of narrow, gun-slit-like windows that looked out onto the woods and the path they had just traveled. Cross and Shanahan stood in front of the second door, waiting for Channing to key in the code.

He pressed the numbers. There was a hissing sound as the double doors parted. Standing in the doorway was an attractive, pregnant black woman. In the quick and startling glimpse she appeared like one of the walking dead. In the split second that Lianna commanded attention, Channing moved back and outside. As Shanahan turned, a sick feeling climbed into his belly. Channing had his electronic key chain in his hand and the front doors were closing. He was smiling broadly.

Both Shanahan and Cross leapt for the narrowing sliver of light, but were too late. When they turned, the door to Lianna had closed as well. The two of them went to the windows. Channing was walking away.

They examined the small room. The narrow slits of windows with glass perhaps two, three inches thick. And even if they were willing to risk a potentially deadly ricochet by trying to shoot them out, the windows were too small for a squirrel to escape. They could probably enter random numbers for a lifetime and never figure out the code to get out or get into the laboratory. There was a ventilator high above the front door. It was too narrow to get through, but there was air . . . and sound.

"Howie, Howie, Howie," Channing said. "You just can't quite get it right."

"He fulfilled his obligation," Cross said. "He took us to the laboratory and showed us Lianna."

Shanahan saw the irony but didn't laugh. Closed spaces frightened him. He looked out one of the windows, saw Channing turn to walk back toward the cabin, no doubt to pack and leave.

Twenty-Seven

What Shanahan saw next was both heartening and frightening. Maureen had stepped into the path in front of Channing. She raised the hunting rifle, aiming it directly at Channing.

"Whoa," Channing said. "What have we here? Annie Oakley?"

Shanahan couldn't see Channing's face, but he guessed the man was smiling. Wrong move, if he did.

"You will turn around and unlock the door," Maureen said.

"I will, huh?"

"If you value various parts of your body."

"It's not loaded, little lady," he said, stepping toward her.

She raised the rifle, shot in the air. The sound echoed against the metal building. He stopped.

"I loaded it." She brought the rifle back to him.

"I see," he said, starting to move toward her. "You're not going to kill anybody."

She stepped back. "I'll ask once more. Stop."

He kept coming.

The sound was deafening and the bullet hit the building. He had ducked, but was too late. He grabbed his left ear, then looked at the blood on his hands.

"Jesus Christ, woman."

"Now, here's how it goes. I take fingers and toes until I get what I want. If you don't play ball, it's knees and elbows. And we'll just keep going from there."

"You shot my ear off," Channing said incredulously.

"Just a tiny piece. It could've been like Van Gogh. Still could, really. I got a lot of bullets left."

Lianna was in the corner, sitting on a cot, waiting. Shanahan and Maureen watched as Cross hog tied Channing and chained him in the bed of his pickup truck.

"You couldn't make it as a cop and you can't make it as a PI," Channing said.

"I guess there's nothing left for me except private security," Cross replied, tightening the knot until Channing yelped. Cross didn't want to take any chances with the wily old ex-cop.

"You know, Channing," Cross said. "A girl took you down."

Lianna had been taken care of. There was food, drink, a full bath, a place to sleep. A television set. For someone who'd been locked away for awhile, she didn't seem in a big hurry to leave, nor did she express any great joy at being rescued.

"It wasn't supposed to be this way," she said, when they returned to gather her things and take her back.

"What way was it supposed to be?" Shanahan asked.

"I was supposed to be able to change my mind," Lianna said. "But when I did, they put me in here."

"We've got time to talk," Shanahan said. "We need to get you home."

"How's Todd?" she asked. "You know him, right?"

"He hired us to find you," Shanahan said. He decided to spare her the whole story. She'd find out soon enough.

Outside, Shanahan asked Howie to call Swann on the cell. When Swann answered, Cross gave Shanahan the phone.

"We've got Lianna," Shanahan said. "And Channing. Why don't you meet us somewhere so you can take him in and announce the good news."

"You what?" Swann asked.

"She's alive and . . . probably well. It's a little rough. I'll fill you in when we meet."

Swann met them in the parking lot of an East Side K-Mart just off I-465, a multi-lane interstate that circled most of

Indianapolis. There were three squad cars, none of them belonging to Lt. Rafferty.

Uniformed cops struggled to get the ropes off Channing.

"That dangerous?" Swann asked Shanahan.

Lianna was huddled in the back seat of Shanahan's Malibu talking with Todd. Shanahan could hear what was being said, but she was crying.

Maureen stood with Shanahan as the elder detective pieced the story together for the lieutenant.

"I want to go with you for the arrest," Shanahan said. "According to Lianna you'll find the culprit at the Indianapolis 500, the owner's suite."

"That's right, the race is today," Cross said, his mind registering the departure date for Margot. The realization that this was it for her added emphasis to his sense that it was over, completely over.

Cross watched as Channing was disentangled and brought to his feet.

Channing looked at him. This wasn't over, Channing seemed to imply with his stare and scowl.

"You can call me 'Howie,'" Cross said. "It's OK. We know each other well enough."

"Howie, baby, you did nothing. Without Ma Barker over there, your ass would be grass."

"I take it anyway I can get it. Think of it this way, you won't have to worry about what to wear or what to fix for dinner for awhile."

Swann apologized, but said he had to take Lianna Bailey in for questioning. He'd have a physician there as well. He'd make her comfortable, he told her. Todd could come down and be with her. But he had a lot of questions.

Shanahan rode with the police. Maureen took Cross home.

Shanahan was there when Rafferty came into the meeting room, where Lianna sat, looking small at the big table.

Swann was with the Police Chief in the Mayor's Office, Rafferty said. Rafferty was being polite with Lianna present.

She was an embarrassment to him, but coming across as the arrogant know-it-all that he was wouldn't help his career. She was a victim all right, but not of Todd Evans, who was clearly a victim as well.

"We're all very glad you've been found alive," Rafferty said. "The entire force, the entire city, has been involved in finding you."

"Why aren't you with the big boys?" Shanahan asked Rafferty.

Rafferty ignored him. It was unclear what Lianna was thinking or feeling. She still had that blank look of someone in shock.

"We'll make every effort," Rafferty continued talking to Lianna, "to make sure Mr. Evans's name is cleared and that the world knows he was inadvertently drawn into the circle of suspicion."

"Circle of suspicion?" Shanahan said. "You guys put him there. All but Swann, a real cop you took off the case."

"Mr. Shanahan, your presence here is through the grace of the police department," Rafferty said. "I think you understand me."

"Ungracious even in defeat," Shanahan said.

"I think we should go," Lianna said touching Shanahan's hand. She stood up.

"You can't go, Miss Bailey," Rafferty said.

"Am I under arrest?" Lianna said curtly, seemingly focused and clear about what was going on around her.

"Of course not," Rafferty said. "We need to have—"

Todd Evans came in the door, followed by James Fenimore Kowalski. He went to Lianna and after that burst of anger and strength, she seemed to collapse in his arms.

"I'm so sorry," she said.

"Don't be sorry. I'm so happy," Todd said.

"I want to go home," she said softly to Todd.

"I'm sorry, Miss Bailey," Rafferty said, "but the case—"

"I think we've all had quite enough of you," Evans said. "Talk to our attorney." He nodded toward Kowalski.

Rafferty looked at Kowalski, who raised an eyebrow. That was all. Rafferty glanced at Shanahan, who kept a straight face, and left the room.

Shanahan rode with Swann. They were followed by three police cars. Because Speedway Indiana is legally a separate town from Indianapolis, despite its proximity, Swann had to run the operation by them and by the Indianapolis 500 security. The police cars, one unmarked, and two marked, moved through the gate, where throngs of people still gathered, descended into a tunnel that went under the two and a half mile oval track, and emerged in the sunlight on the other side.

On the inside of the track were a full eighteen-hole golf course and several towers in addition to the garages for the thirty-three cars entered into the race. On the other side the track were hundreds of thousands of spectators watching as cars raced at well over 200 miles per hour.

Swann drove toward a six-story building that looked like it belonged in Japan. It was called "the Pagoda." In it were the ritziest of suites where one could view the start and finish line in quiet, air-conditioned comfort.

The owner's suite occupied the top two floors. They went to Suite 2, a rather plain name for a place that was clearly on the right side of the tracks. Inside the fifth floor—done contemporarily in chrome and leather with walls of rich olive green, burnt orange and mustard—were a hundred or so folks in golf shirts and khakis dining on food that ranged from hot dogs to tenderloin in what appeared to be some sort of fruit sauce.

Swann and Shanahan scanned the room, while two of the uniformed police stationed themselves at the door. Not finding who they wanted, the two of them moved out onto the balcony that overlooked the track. One could hear the searing noise of the cars as they went past. There were maybe three dozen out there, none of them the person they were looking for.

Shanahan and Cross, along with two uniformed police officers went through the crowd and upstairs, causing a wave of whispers that turned into a buzz. People looked concerned, but no one interfered or asked questions.

Upstairs was the bar. Widescreen TVs were scattered about, on walls and in corners. Across the room, where people drank champagne, beer, and mixed drinks, there was another balcony, identical to the one below.

Shanahan saw Pedersen. He motioned for Swann to follow. Pedersen noticed them right away, gave them a stern look as they approached. Pedersen broke with his group to cut them off.

"What is this all about?" he asked Swann. "Are you making a deliberate attempt to embarrass me? And you?" Pedersen turned to Shanahan. "What do I have to do to keep you from interfering in my life?"

"Tell us where Mary Beth Schmidt is."

"What?"

"She's here, right?"

Pedersen, still agitated and looking around, replied. "Yes, somewhere. What is this all about?"

"We found Lianna," Swann said.

Pedersen looked surprised, but also relieved. "Oh, thank God," he said, almost losing his breath. "Is she all right?"

"She'll be fine," Shanahan said. "She's carrying your child, or your brother, or maybe, depending on how you look at it, she's carrying you."

"What on earth are you talking about?"

"Lianna Bailey is carrying your clone, Mr. Pedersen," Swann said.

Shanahan recognized Mary Beth Schmidt, who had come toward the balcony and then halted and turned. Shanahan made his way after her. She started toward the door, saw the policeman posted there and stopped again. She turned, looking both confused and desperate.

"Miss Schmidt?"

"Yes," she tried hard to pull herself together.

"We've got Channing."
She nodded.
"We have Lianna Bailey," Shanahan continued.
She nodded again.
"We know."
"She agreed," Mary Beth Schmidt said. "She wanted to. We made this incredible investment. And it worked. It worked. It was going to happen the way we planned."
"She changed her mind, right?"
Mary Beth Schmidt nodded.
"And Pedersen?"
"He didn't know."
"All of that money for the laboratory? All that time away. Whatever else all of this may cost? You're saying he didn't know?"
Something must have happened on the track because there was a sudden stilling of the partygoers and a rush to the balcony and to the television sets.
"No. I had quite a bit of latitude in developing the technology in advance of what we all believed would be an eventual go-ahead in clone development. He knew we were setting up a lab in a quiet corner of the state and that we were doing some basic animal work. He had no idea we were as far along as we were."
"But you used him," Shanahan said.
"Why wouldn't we?" she asked. "Look at him. Good looking, incredibly healthy, as bright as they come?"
"You're saying those teeth are for real?"
She looked at him as if he were an ant that crawled on her picnic potato salad.

Twenty-Eight

Shanahan, once the arrest was over, went home. It was four in the afternoon, but it seemed more like midnight. He was exhausted, emotionally, physically, spiritually.

Maureen had picked up a pizza for an early dinner. Conversation between them was polite but sparse. Neither wanted to discuss anything. Even Casey seemed to have had enough of the day. He declined a trip to the backyard. Instead he sat at Maureen's feet in the living room.

The phone rang. Shanahan was already on his feet, so he went to the kitchen to answer it. Jennifer Bailey was on the other line.

"I'm so very sorry," she said.

"Don't worry about it."

"I'm afraid I've abused my power. Worse, I've abused my friend. Will you forgive me?"

"Of course. I don't think very many of us get through life without doing something we thought was right, but wasn't. I've done my share. And I hope I've been forgiven." His thoughts were on his son and his family.

"It's a wonderful thing you've done, Mr. Shanahan. I guess I've learned not to doubt you. I owe you."

"You owe me nothing," he said. He wanted it all to go away.

"They're very happy," she said. "Thing is, of course, it's not over."

Shanahan understood, but he didn't want to get into it. There was the whole idea of a cloned human carried in the process of coming to life. And among those most horrified at the

208

prospect of cloning are the very people who believe that abortion is murder. What would they have Lianna do? It was very tiring.

"They're young," Shanahan told her. "Somehow they will get through it."

"I hope you're right," Jennifer Bailey said. "I had no idea you were an optimist after all."

"For now," he said. "In self-defense."

"All right. I'll let you off the hook. For tonight, anyway. Thank you," she said, and hung up.

Cross settled into his sofa, pleasantly tired, clicking a few channels to see if there was something that would catch his eye. Nothing did, but it was all right. He might have felt worse if there wasn't some sense of satisfaction about the day's events. It wasn't just seeing Channing hog-tied in the back of his own pickup truck, which went a long way to relieve his sense of retribution, though that was significant in and of itself. It was that Lianna was found—alive. He had held no hope for such a turn of events. He was relieved too that Margot left. She was now beyond his reach, beyond temptation—for awhile.

There was also the possibility that he might get paid. Kowalski had told Shanahan that he was going to squeeze some money out of the city for the false arrest. He said that when he did he would spread it around.

Maybe he could get on with his life. Of course, he'd have to figure out what that meant. Getting on.

The morning was brighter for Shanahan. The sun was distant, but golden. He felt a wisp of a breeze as the wooden screen door opened squeakily. Casey let himself out into the back yard, and the door slammed shut behind him. Shanahan had rested well. If he dreamed during the night, he didn't remember. If he got up for his usual 3 A.M. trip to the bathroom, he didn't remember that either.

Maureen was still asleep, as was her custom.

Shanahan made coffee, fed Einstein, and opened the

morning paper. Yesterday's drama wasn't mentioned. Apparently, no one at the Indianapolis 500 suite bothered to alert the media. He was about to go to the living room to switch on TV to see if they had anything, when the phone rang.

"Swann here," the voice said.

"What's up?"

"Press conference at eleven this morning. You want to come?"

"Nope."

"You sure? Your moment to shine."

"Who is going to be there?"

"The Chief, Lianna, Todd, Mr. Kowalski, and me."

"Rafferty?"

"They sent him over to Ripley County to pick up Channing's belongings."

Shanahan tried to catch either gloating or humor in Swann's tone. He said it as if he were reading a stock report.

"And Mary Beth and Channing?"

"Channing is easy. Kidnapping, conspiracy to commit a crime. Mary Beth? They're trying to figure out the charge. Kidnapping? Sure. Conspiracy? Yep. But what about taking someone's skin cell and uh . . . what do they call it? . . . replicating human beings without their permission? Is that theft?"

"Someday, that will be a patent violation or copyright infringement," Shanahan said. "Seems to be the way the world is going."

"In the meantime, we're stuck."

"You shave yet?" Shanahan asked.

"I did. My little world is back to normal," he said.

Shanahan looked down on the kitchen table. There were several brochures—"Ten Nights in Tuscany," "Venice for Lovers," "Your Roman Holiday," "The Riviera, Italian Style."

"I spent a couple of decades in normal. But there's no hope I'll ever return."

"OK," Swann said. "Listen." There was a long pause. The

straight-laced cop of few words was formulating a complex sentence perhaps. "Thanks."

Maureen stumbled into the kitchen, drowsier than usual. She squinted at the world.

Shanahan poured her a cup of coffee, handed it to her.

"Guaranteed to restore perkiness."

"I'm not perky. I've never been perky. I will never be perky," she said in a scolding manner. "You may not use the word 'perky' in my presence."

She went to the kitchen table, pushed away the brochures to make room for the coffee cup, and sat.

"What's wrong?"

"What are they going to do with the baby?" Maureen asked.

Shanahan couldn't help thinking that the baby was the proto-type of an entirely new corporate product line. But he'd keep his thoughts to himself.

"Have you figured out where we're going?" Shanahan asked.

She took a deep breath, looked at Shanahan.

"You really are ready, willing, and eager to go?"

"I am all of those things. At least."

"Hmmm. I'm starting to feel just a little perky."

Twenty-Nine

"We are very pleased to tell you that Lianna Bailey has been found, a little the worse for wear, but unharmed." The Indianapolis Police Department's chief of police talked directly into the camera. Shanahan, who watched on the bedroom TV set, along with Maureen, thought he looked like he could be a bank clerk. A nice looking, but plain man appeared. His face showed none of the toughness it would take to rise through the ranks.

"We have apprehended two suspects in the kidnapping," the Chief continued. "We will be providing you with additional information. We are very thankful for the efforts of our citizens in the apprehension of those responsible. We are also deeply sorry for any inconvenience we might have caused an innocent man."

"*Might* have caused?" Maureen said.

"I want to introduce Mr. James Kowalski," the Chief said, looking suddenly uncomfortable, "who has something to say about his client Todd Evans, who was, for some time, a person of interest."

"He was *arrested*," Maureen said to the television.

"He can't hear you. You know that, right?"

Maureen gave Shanahan a dirty look. "You talk to the Cubs manager every time there's a game."

"I never utter a word," Shanahan said.

"You grunt and curse and sometimes act quite nasty."

"For several days," Kowalski began, "a member of the Indianapolis Police Department painted a picture of a guilty man constructed entirely of innuendo, circumstantial evidence, and spin. The media, not doing its job to investigate and provide checks and balances to government authority, permitted . . . no enabled . . . the near destruction of a fine young man who was already suffering because of her disappearance.

"I am not asking for resignations, or additional apologies, or any kind of retribution. Perhaps the city can provide some assistance to the young man and his fiancée. However, what I want to come out of this is that lessons are learned. That both the media and public figures not permit either a sensational story or the influence of the powerful to keep them from the obligations they have to the public.

"Todd and Lianna will try and I am sure they will succeed to put their lives back together. In the meantime, the story that needs to be told is how this injustice was allowed to exist.

"Thank you."

As the cameras cut away to an on-the-scene news reporter, Shanahan heard the shouts of questions from other reporters that weren't answered.

"Mr. Kowalski," said the fair-haired man with the microphone, "has made an eloquent plea for understanding the trials and tribulations that await the newly reunited couple—"

Shanahan clicked off the set.

"Lessons learned," he said.

"We're done here, right?" Maureen said, standing.

"Yep."

Thirty

Howie found a letter and a small package in his mailbox. Quite a bonanza for someone who only received bills and advertisements. He considered, for a moment, that the package might be a letter bomb from Channing. There was no return address, but it was postmarked in San Francisco. The letter was postmarked in Cleveland.

He opened the letter first as he walked back through the gate toward his front door.

Cross sat on the bench on his front porch and read the letter.

> Howie,
>
> A short note to let you know that on average we had fun times. I think we helped each other for awhile. But this last round was a little painful for both of us. You have to know by now that I'm pretty bad at being good. I'll be back through Indianapolis from time to time, at least until I get too old for the circuit. If we happen to run into each other, let us just smile and wave and keep on going. It will be better that way.
>
> Love,
> M

He crumpled the letter and started to throw it. He put it in his pocket instead. He looked down at the package. "OK, it's only up from here," he said to his empty yard.

He opened it. It was a CD.

Out of the Cage was the title. There was a photograph of

a blonde-again Nina Moore. She looked happy being sad, Cross thought. He wondered how she did it.

Maureen and Shanahan sat in the late-morning sun outside a little café in Florence. Maureen sipped slowly the glass of red wine and gazed out at the passersby. Shanahan, with a coffee and pastry, let his eyes wander across the facades of centuries-old buildings.

He thought he hadn't really stepped back in time as much as he was given a position in it. As old as it all was, it was not old at all. And as old as he was, he was not old in any real sense, just close to his own, personal end. Maureen was either constructing a plan for dinner, admiring the stylish Italians, or perhaps eyeing a young, romantic Italian man.

He believed she was not contemplating time—and that was good. It was, in many ways, silly for him to do so. But what does one do at this point in his life but measure time? It is the reverse of being ten and wanting to be twenty-one. That was a slow, slow process. On this side of it, time accelerated. And for him, now, he wanted to push back against the inevitable.

On the other hand, Shanahan thought, he was not mentally constructed for this cold new era. Cell-phone and internet relationships. He could understand the manned trips into space, but he was in an absolutely confused state about humans engineering future humans. He had no opinion, which perplexed him. He knew too that his opinion, even if he had one, wouldn't matter.

It was not his world anymore. It simply wasn't.

"What are you thinking?" Maureen asked.

"How beautiful you are," he said.

"Your lies are always welcomed."

In a way, he was, just as he had before he met Maureen, just passing time. No longer engaged in most of the world's offerings. Only now, with Maureen, the wait was more pleasant and the eventual departure more profound.

215

The sun glanced off Maureen's wineglass and he returned to the moment. As the waiter went by, he called out.

"A glass of wine, please," he said, nodding toward Maureen's. "Make that two."